THE PROSPECT

A LONG BALL BOYS NOVELLA

LYSSA KAY ADAMS

Dear Reader,

The original version of The Prospect appeared exclusively in a 2017 boxset called The Hot Zone, which is no longer available. So I am releasing my novella as a stand-alone title!

I hope you enjoy Jax and Bree's story! It's just the beginning for The Long Ball Boys...

~ Lyssa

PROLOGUE

Two summers ago

JAX TANNER

SHE DANCES ON THE SHORE, a lone dark shape against the moonlit lake, a silhouette hidden by the shifting swell of the sand.

From the top of the dunes, I see the massive bonfire rising from the beach a hundred yards away, illuminating the throbbing surge of drunken, dancing teenagers who graduated from the local high school earlier in the day, including her.

She's one of them but not. She stands apart. Alone.

I'm not supposed to be here. None of my teammates are. The rules are strict when you're a first-year player for the Silver Lake Sluggers—the elite summer baseball team for the nation's best college players like me. Curfew is at midnight and underage drinking is forbidden. You break the rules, and you're out. No questions asked.

It sucks to think about spending my summer like a monk, but it's such a privilege to be invited to play for the Sluggers—or any team in the prestigious Mackinac League—that we accept it. Just putting on a Sluggers uniform sends your stock soaring and tells the entire baseball world you're the real deal.

A Major League hopeful.

A *prospect*.

But here I am, on the verge of breaking the rules, cresting one of the famous Silver Lake sand dunes with midnight less than an hour away, because I heard *she* would be here. The girl who works in the kitchen at the team boarding house.

The one who has been shooting me shy smiles for two weeks while she refills the salad bowl or brushes past me in the dining room. The one whose amber-brown eyes shimmer with a sadness she can never fully conceal. The one whose hips now sway to her own hypnotic rhythm that sucks me in like a powerful riptide.

Her arms are aloft in a graceful arch over her head. Her long, dark hair blows in the breeze. A beer loosely dangles from her fingertips, forgotten, an afterthought. Like the entire beach party raging without her in the distance.

Sand fills my shoes as I descend the hill. My teammates leave me in search of their own diversions, but I head for her. Only her.

"Bree," I say, testing her name on the breeze.

She turns, arms falling to her sides and her beer dropping to the wet ground at her feet. Her eyes widen and her lips part. I should probably say something, anything, but I can't.

"You're not supposed to be here," she blurts.

"I know," I laugh.

"You'll get in trouble if they catch you."

"I know."

"Then why are you…"

Her question disappears as I extend my hand. She stares at it with cautious longing—the same expression I catch on her face when she thinks I'm not paying attention. But I am. I always am.

"When was the last time someone told you you're the most beautiful girl in the world?"

"N-never."

"That ends today."

Bree slowly reaches out. I fold her fingers in mine and tug her closer.

I might be a fool for being here.

For breaking the rules.

For risking everything.

But when she locks her eyes with mine and gives me that shy smile, I know it's going to be worth it.

The right girl always is.

1

Two summers later

BREE MCTAVISH

"GIVE ME THAT BRA, or I swear to God, I'll cook you."

This is how it's going to end for me. In a face-off with a ten-pound ball of white fluff and sass. Everything I've worked for, every hour spent learning the ropes in a hot kitchen, every moment spent sweating the small stuff in my bank account until it's just big enough to get out of this town. *Poof.* It's all going to disappear because of this hoarding, mocking thief who's smirking at me because she knows she can get away with it. She's the pampered princess of the boarding house owner whose goodwill can change in the blink of an eye, and I'm nothing but a cook who can be sent packing just as fast.

I swear she plans these things, this dog. It's like she waits for me to turn my back so she can dart underfoot at just the wrong moment to force me to spill a bowl of carefully washed cherries or knock over a tray of fresh muffins.

Or, in this case, so she can scamper into the butler's pantry and emerge with evidence of the secret I hide behind the shelves of canned tomatoes, pancake mixes, and apocalypse-sized jars of vegetable oil.

I love dogs. I do. If I didn't have my heart set on a career as a professional chef, I'd do something with animals. Because I love them.

Just not this one.

And definitely not today. Because today is *the* day. The day the Sluggers move back into Edsel House for another summer of stealing bases and hearts. The day my hometown loses its damn mind over the aptly nicknamed Long Ball Boys.

Most importantly, the day *he* returns for his last summer here.

I should be rushing through my prep work for tomorrow's team breakfast so I can escape to a safe hiding space and start the agonizing process of avoiding Jax Tanner for another three long months.

But what am I doing instead? I'm chasing Miss Matilda around the stainless-steel counters and appliances of the massive, professional-grade kitchen to retrieve the embarrassingly small scrap of faded pink lace now caught in her teeth.

Miss Matilda skids to her right. I try to grab her, but I realize too late it was a fake. She veers left around the prep counter and toward the door … which suddenly swings open from the other side. My non-existent career flashes before my eyes as I imagine Mrs. Armitage, owner of the house, or Mrs. C—the head cook —walking in.

Instead, I let out a relieved breath as my best friend, Lexi Acevedo, strolls in. "Shut the door!" I squawk.

Lexi nearly drops the paper bag in her arms, whips around and grabs the handle to stop the door from swinging. Matilda growls, races between her legs, and picks up the chase again.

"What the hell is going on?" Lexi laughs, setting the bag on the prep island in the center of the kitchen. The bag tips, and a bundle of fresh asparagus tumbles out with a clump of dirt from her mom's garden.

I run to the door and stand in the jamb, arms and legs splayed to block anyone else from coming in. "She stole my bra!"

Lexi looks under the counter and bursts out laughing. "How did she get your bra?"

"I did a load of laundry here," I lie, instantly feeling guilty for the deception. I hate lying to Lexi.

"At least she didn't grab your underwear."

"Get one of her treats and see if she'll come to you."

"Right," she snorts. "That dog hates me as much as she hates you."

True. Lexi and I have both been working at Edsel House since the summer before our senior year in high school, and Matilda has always treated us like a couple of hussies after her boyfriend. She's a bona fide mean girl. If she could shove us in front of a bus, she would.

But the men? Oh, she *loves* them. The instant a Slugger comes within twenty feet of her, she's on her back, showing her belly, begging for snuggles. And they fall for it every time. Every muscled alpha male on the team turns into a slobbering ball of mush over that damn dog.

Who has now inched out from under the counter to taunt me.

The little brat planned this just for today. I know it.

Lexi rises and shoots me a look over her shoulder. "Just stop chasing her. She'll let go of it the minute it stops being a game."

"It's not a game to her. She wants to ruin me."

Lexi makes a cuckoo noise and starts unpacking her bag. "My mom wants to know if you need any more morels. She's taking another tour out tomorrow morning."

I abandon my blockade of the door with a strong glare at Matilda. "If she can find them this late in the season, I'll cook them."

Lexi's mom owns a local hair salon but moonlights as a morel mushroom hunter, which sounds whacko to most people but not when you're from around here. This part of Michigan is a tourist destination for foodies who savor the nutty-flavored fungus that grows in the soggy forest floors just after the spring thaw.

"So..." Lexi says too casually, running asparagus under the water in the sink.

"Don't say it," I grumble.

"I saw him when I was walking in."

"I told you not to say it."

"He looks good."

Of course, he does. He couldn't *not* look good. He's the *satisfaction guaranteed* of hotness, and ever since the night of my graduation, I've had to suffer his sexiness every summer as punishment for my own stupidity and recklessness.

I was kind of hoping he wouldn't come this year.

Yet I'm shamefully giddy he did.

Just one more reason I can't wait to get out of Silver Lake, my tiny hometown where the only thing more famous than the blowing sand of the dunes is the annual antics of the Sluggers. They didn't get the nickname "The Long Ball Boys" for nothing. Girls who grow up here learn two unbreakable lessons: how to properly cook morels and how to not lose your heart to a Long Baller.

I mastered the first one under careful instruction.

Too bad I had to learn the second one the hard way.

But I only have three more months of this, and then I'll have enough money to get out. Michigan's capital city awaits with its renowned community college culinary program. It's not exactly *Le Cordon Bleu*, but a girl with no connections and zero money has to start somewhere. I've been working my ass off for a long, long time to start there.

"He's, like, different or something," Lexi continues, gently shaking the asparagus of excess water and me of my wandering thoughts.

"Different how?"

She shrugs. "Bigger. Or maybe taller. I don't know. It's just something. It's like he went from hot to *holy shit* in a single year. You'll have to see for yourself."

"No thanks."

Lexi adopts a sing-song voice. "He has a beard."

My lady parts clench. A beard on Jax Tanner? Fate really does hate me.

"Not, like, one of those gross long ones," Lexi says, and we both shudder. The rest of the world may have fallen in love with that whole lumbersexual thing, but we've grown up around national forest rangers who need to keep their faces warm in the winter, and we know for a fact how unsanitary that shit is.

"It's one of those sexy short ones that you can't tell if he grew on purpose or just got too lazy to shave for a while," Lexi says. "Like the kind you want to just scratch with your fingernails."

I know the kind she's talking about, and picturing it on Jax's jawline has me fanning myself.

Lexi snorts. "That's what I thought."

I've never denied an attraction to him. I'm just trying to be smart enough not to act on it again.

Matilda races toward me, trying to get back in the game. I take Lexi's advice and ignore her. Matilda starts shaking my bra like she's trying to kill it, and she'll probably succeed. It's a three-year-old clearance aisle special that only has a few more washes in it before total disintegration.

Which feels like a sad metaphor for my life.

I bundle the freshly cleaned asparagus with some loose kitchen twine and prop it in a shallow dish of water. Best way to keep it fresh for tomorrow night's dinner.

Lexi returns to the prep counter to clean up the dirt. "Oh," she says, stopping to dig into her pocket. She pulls out a folded yellow paper. "Mom also wanted me to tell you that you're entering this year, no matter what, and if you say no, she's never going to give you another mushroom again."

I take the paper and shove it in my own pocket without looking at it. I know what it is. It's the entry form for the annual recipe contest at the upcoming International Asparagus Festival, which is actually a thing because *Michigan*.

Lexi side-eyes me on the way back to the sink. "The judges are big-time this year. You could get noticed by someone important."

"I'll think about it."

"But the deadline is in three days!"

"So, I'll think about it until then."

Lexi plants her hands on her hips and gives me the look—the one she's been giving me since middle school when she knows I'm holding something back. That look has gotten me to confess way too much over the years, which is why I'm looking everywhere but at her right now. The secret I'm hiding today is way too humiliating, and her mom will just try to help me. *Again.* I already owe them both too much.

"You know you're good enough to win," Lexi says.

"I know." I'm not being conceited. I'm talented in the kitchen, especially for someone with no formal training. Desperation is an efficient tutor. I've even started picking up gigs as a local wedding caterer on top of my work at the Edsel House. The extra money is the only reason I'm going to be able to get out of this town at the end of this summer instead of next.

But just barely, which is why the contest is once again not going to happen. I don't have an extra two hundred and fifty dollars to cover the entry fee.

Lexi sighs like she's about to lecture me, but she cuts it off when we hear the voice.

His voice.

In the dining room and coming closer.

I can't make out the words, but it sounds like he's on the phone with someone. I hear the deep timbre of his low laugh, and a shiver races up my spine as I imagine a hot blonde on the other side of the call. Or a hot brunette. Or just any other girl, because he could totally have a girlfriend and probably does by now. And I hate myself for caring.

I close my eyes and swallow as an entire kaleidoscope of butterflies takes flight in my stomach.

Lexi slugs me on the arm. "Go out there and say hi."

I slug back. "No."

"If you won't, I will."

She starts for the door. I grab her arm to hold her back, but she sticks her tongue out at me and pulls away.

Disaster unfolds in slow motion, like one of those dreams where you need to run but can't get your feet to move.

Lexi plants her hand in the center of the swinging door.

"Lexi, wait!"

But it's too late. Matilda has spotted her escape. She races out from under the counter. The door starts to swing shut again, but Matilda manages to slip through the tiny sliver of opening and out of sight, straight into the dining room, my bra dangling from her mouth like a dead animal.

This really is where it ends for me. Because the only thing more embarrassing than the sound of Jax's amused laughter as he greets the little brat is the look on his face when he pushes the door open from the other side, my bra dangling from his fingers.

He holds it out and quirks an eyebrow over sexy, hooded eyes. "What exactly do you do in this kitchen, Bree?"

2

BREE

LEXI WAS RIGHT. He's one hundred percent *holy shit.*

My brain tries to catalogue all the changes during the split-second suspension of time between my irrational dizziness at seeing him and my total humiliation at the circumstances. He's bigger. Broader. He fills up the space in the doorway like a ... well, like a full-grown *man.* But it's not just his sheer size that has changed. There's something about his eyes, too. He swings the bra and cocks an eyebrow over a carefully schooled expression. He has looked at me many ways over the past two years—shyly, seductively, apologetically—but never like this. Never mockingly.

I recover from my stupor long enough to stomp two steps closer and grab my bra. I shove it in my pocket. Matilda, who has settled between his feet like she's guarding a prize, growls and bares her teeth.

Don't worry, dog. He's all yours.

Lexi clears her throat in a totally non-subtle way. "Hey, Jax," she chirps. "How was school this year?"

He glances her way. "Good. You?"

Lexi attends Michigan State. "Great. It was, um, great." Lexi bites her lip and then swivels on her feet to stare at me. She bugs out her eyes at me as if to say, *Say something.*

"Did-did you need something?" I stammer.

He pats his stomach. "Yeah, I'm starving. I missed dinner. I was going to grab an apple or something, but then Matilda tried to give me a present." He winks. *Winks.* Not in a meaningful way, either, but in an empty, flirty way. I hate it.

Correction. I hate *myself.*

"Anyway, don't suppose you have anything left over from dinner?"

"A little."

"Awesome. Mind if I fix a plate?"

"I-I can do it."

"Really? Thanks."

He winks again, and the hollow gesture makes heat rise on my skin. I walk toward the line of commercial refrigerators that take up nearly an entire wall of the kitchen. I avoid Lexi's gaze, because everything about this is humiliating. The way he's treating me. My bra. Everything.

I open the first fridge and pull out a stack of three dishes of left-over chicken, mashed potatoes, and gravy. I set them on the prep counter and then retrieve a warm plate from the dishwasher on the other side of the refrigerators.

"Looks awesome," he says, coming up next to me as I return to the prep counter. He peers over my shoulder. "I swear, you need to write a cookbook or something. You know that chicken dish you started making last year? The one with the cherry barbeque sauce?

I tried to make that for my girlfriend, but I didn't even come close."

Girlfriend. My hand shakes, and I dribble gravy on the counter as I transfer it from bowl to plate. Lexi is suddenly super busy doing absolutely nothing.

I slide the plate in his direction without turning around. "You can use the microwave in the dining room."

He grabs the plate. "Thanks, Bree. You're the best."

And then he turns and walks back through the door.

My hands rest on the cold counter. I'm stunned into mute inertia. *Thanks, Bree. You're the best.* Did he really just say that? After dropping the girlfriend bomb in my lap? The heat on my cheeks explodes from the mild burn of embarrassment to a raging inferno of mortification. In all my years working here, I've never felt more like the hired help than I do right now.

"Bree," Lexi sighs, waving a hand in front of my face from the other side of the counter.

I shake my head. "Don't."

"I'm sure it's not a serious girlfriend."

"He cooked for her." *Using one of my recipes.* "That's a serious girlfriend."

"Well, what did you expect? You've been blowing him off for two years! Anyone would give up after that."

"I haven't been blowing him off."

"Yes, you have. I've never seen a guy so hung up on a girl before. I actually felt sorry for him last year."

"You don't understand."

"You're right. I don't. He's hot. Why not take advantage—"

"I had sex with him," I blurt.

Lexi blinks so hard and fast that she looks like one of those annoying talking bird dolls we were obsessed with as kids. The ones you had to tiptoe around when you got up in the middle of the night to pee because the slightest vibration would send it squawking awake for an hour.

"I'm sorry, I think I just hallucinated. Did you say you had sex with him? With Jax Tanner?!"

The last part came out a high-pitched squeak. I hiss at her. "Keep your voice down!"

Lexi rounds the counter and grabs my arm to shake me. "When the hell did this happen?" She doesn't wait for me to answer. I see the conclusion arrive in her eyes as she steps back. "Holy shit. The night on the beach. After graduation."

I nod, avoiding her eyes by repacking the left-overs.

"How could you not tell me?"

"I didn't want you to know."

"*Why*? You're my best friend! That's the whole point of having a best friend, so you have someone to tell when you lose your virginity to a hot guy on a beach!"

"I know, but—"

"I told you when I lost my virginity last summer! How could you not at least *mention* it?"

"Because I didn't want you to know what an idiot I am!"

Lexi sighs again and leans against the counter. She doesn't need me to clarify what I mean. Lexi is walking, breathing proof of what happens when a local girl violates Rule Number Two.

The town's favorite game next to baseball itself is guessing which Major League ball player is Lexi's father. Everyone knows she's the product of a summer fling between a local girl with stars in her eyes and a Long Baller with lust in his who then took off at summer's end and never looked back.

That's probably why we became friends. We both walk around this town with giant gossip targets on our backs. The only thing they love to talk about as much as the identity of Lexi's father is the ugly truth about mine.

"You're done with school now, and you're no longer my responsibility."

I stare at the suitcase he dropped at my feet. The graduation cap slides off my head. "You're my father!"

"You're an adult now. Grow up and have a nice life."

I shake off the memory. It doesn't matter. I'm over it.

"Bree, I wouldn't have judged you. Is that what you think?" Lexi asks.

I shrug and return the dishes to the fridge.

"I would never judge you! And anyway, he's not like the others. He's not like my sperm donor. Jax seems like a good guy. And he was so into you!"

I shove the dishes back in the fridge and turn around, arms crossed. "It doesn't matter now."

She leans against the counter and matches my pose. "So, what happened?"

"I threw myself at him."

Lexi covers her mouth with her hand, but not before I see her smile.

"Laugh, if you want, but it's true. It was all me. He invited me to go for a walk, we stopped to sit and talk in that little patch of birch trees by the dunes, and the next thing I know, we're going at it like monkeys."

Lexi laughs but stops herself. "I'm sorry. It's just so not you. Were you drunk?"

"No. Just—" I shrug and give her a pointed look. "You know."

"Upset," she says quietly. She was the one who picked me up after Brett—I refuse to think of him as Dad—threw me out with my meager belongings stuffed into that suitcase.

"So, was it, like, bad or something?"

It's my turn to laugh. "Uh, no. It was amazing."

Perfect, actually. Passionate. Romantic. What every girl dreams her first time will be like—a fairy tale under a full moon. But like any good fairy tale, the clock struck midnight.

"Then I don't understand why—"

"Because I knew better, you know? How many times did your mom warn us not to trust a Long Baller? I tried to tell myself I was just using him for sex, but when it was over, I knew it wasn't going to be enough for me. I wanted more." I shrug. "So, I ran."

"Before he could run away from you."

I nod. Sometimes she knows me better than I know myself.

"He doesn't seem to be running, though. He's back for a third summer, Bree."

"With a *girlfriend*. He's not back for me."

"What if he was?"

"It wouldn't matter. I'm smarter than that. Brett didn't teach me much, but he did make me grow up. I have too much at stake to waste my time on some childish, romantic fantasy. No matter how good he looks in a beard."

Lexi closes the small distance between us and pulls me in for a tight hug. "I still can't believe you didn't tell me. I'm trying really hard to not hate you for that."

"I'm sorry." I squeeze my arms around her, guilt rising again because of what else I'm keeping from her right now.

Lexi pulls away. "It's OK. I just worry about you sometimes, you know?"

"You're becoming your mother," I tease.

"I know. And I'm going tell you exactly what she would tell you. It's awesome to plan for the future and all that, but don't forget to live your life, too."

"I'll try to remember that the next time he wants to have sex with me." Which is going to be never, obviously. Because girlfriend.

Lexi shrugs. "Why not? Use him for sex and live in the moment. Maybe a meaningless summer fling is exactly what you need."

"I don't know how to do meaningless."

"Easy. Just keep your heart out of it."

Right. Easy.

Lexi laughs and heads for the door. "I gotta run. See you tomorrow."

The annual pre-season team dinner is tomorrow night. Lexi always helps cook and serve. I wave as she leaves. As soon as she's gone, I drop my face into my hands.

Three more months.

That's all I have left until I can start over in a place where I don't need to hide behind secrets. Where I don't see the look of pity on every face I meet. Where I'm no longer reminded of a Prince Charming and his smile on a moonlit beach.

Three months.

And then I can finally start writing my own damn happy ending.

3

JAX

EVERYONE IS AVOIDING ME.

Move-in night at the Edsel House is an important ritual. The team gets together without coaches to initiate the newest players. As a senior-level player, the young guys should be crowded around me with awe-struck looks on their faces.

But they're all keeping their distance from me. Despite a dearth of seating, I've been allowed to occupy an entire couch by myself while others splay out on the floor to play Nintendo Classic. Those brave enough to say *hi* quickly shift their eyes away, as if staring at my face will turn them to stone. I wish I could pretend it's because I'm putting out a keep-away vibe over what happened in the kitchen with Bree, but I'm not stupid.

Baseball players are superstitious as fuck. Win a big game? Then you'd better wear the same socks every single game after that.

Smash a major heater over the wall? Figure out whatever your coach said to you before you walked to the plate and make sure he says it every time.

But fall into a run of bad luck? Then back the fuck up, because that shit is contagious.

And right now, I'm Patient Fucking Zero.

I tip my beer back and suck down the rest of it. Might as well get started. My life may be a grand-slam catastrophe, but tonight is a big deal for the first-timers, and it's up to the older players like me to introduce them to the traditions that have made the Long Ball Boys a tight-knit fraternity for three generations.

I wander to the front of the room, stepping over bodies as I go. A couple of guys are feeding treats to Matilda. I glare at her. *Damn dog.*

My teammate Grady Cutler, an Oregon State player who's here for his second summer, joins me.

"Everyone shut up," he orders.

The room goes silent. Being a senior-level player brings a certain level of hero-worship from the younger guys, with or without a curse on your back. I remember the first night of my first year, looking up to the older guys whose names and amateur careers I'd followed for years as if they were gods.

I remember, too, the first time I saw *her* the next morning.

Which, fuck, is not something I want to think about right now. I drag my hand down my face. The rookies stare at me like I'm nuts.

That's right, kids. Take a good long look. This is what can happen. One day you're a Top 20 prospect and a guaranteed first-round draft pick with a multi-million dollar signing bonus on the horizon. The next, you slip on a patch of ice and you're lying on a cold sidewalk, your shoulder screaming, and your status dropping somewhere near *maybe*.

Suddenly, I'm a wait-and-see. A probably-not-this-year.

Everyone tells me it's all going to be OK. That I still have another year at Ohio State left. That if I don't get drafted this year, it will happen next year. Probably.

They don't understand.

In baseball, you're nothing but a product. No team wants to buy a broken player. One more year of college isn't going to fix that.

I shake my head. Gotta get my mind back in this game. "Rookies, stand up."

They obey like military recruits. I half expect them to salute.

"Raise your right hands."

Seven right hands go in the air, along with two left ones. Grady snorts and rolls his eyes. Every fucking year, someone fails the test.

"Kincaid and Ruiz," Grady says, calling them out. "In honor of your special brand of dumb-fuckery, you two get first-week bathroom duty on the dormer floor."

They look around confused until they realize their mistake. They switch hands quickly.

"Repeat after me," I say. "I, state your name."

The room shakes with a collection of shouted names.

"Hereby solemnly swear to uphold the traditions of being a Long Baller."

Half of them mangle it, but I plow forward.

"To play my fucking balls off."

That one they get right.

"And to listen to my coaches and the seniors when I'm being an asshat."

They mostly manage that one.

I nod, and they lower their hands. "Now for the house rules. No underage drinking. In by midnight. And under no circumstances, and I mean no fucking way, are you to bother the girl in the kitchen."

Grady looks over at me, eyebrows raised.

"I mean it. She's off-fucking-limits. Any of you fuckers say anything to upset her or make her do extra work for you or do anything other than kiss her ass for putting up with you, I will personally kick you off this team. Leave her the fuck alone."

Silence greets my words. Maybe I really am nuts.

I head to the wide, open doors that lead to a stone terrace outside. I grab another beer in a cooler by the door and walk out. The terrace stretches the entire length of the house and sits high atop a tiered staircase that leads to a private stretch of beach below.

The stone balustrade is cool beneath my arms as I lean. The first time I came here and saw this view, I got a fucking hard-on from the sheer luck of it. While guys on other summer teams are sweating their balls off in college dorm rooms or enduring awkward dinners with host families, I get to live here. In an historic mansion with a private beach.

But there's not much to feel lucky about this year. The view only adds to the creeping sense of panic I can't seem to shake. I should have listened to my coach back at Ohio State. He wanted to send me to the Cape Cod League this summer to get me in front of different scouts for the few weeks leading up to the draft.

Just in case, he said. Which was short-hand for *just in case a miracle happens and someone decides to look past the minor shoulder injury that sidelined me for half the college season.*

I told him no, though. I told him I wanted to play for the Sluggers coach again. That I'm part of the Long Ball Boys for life.

I might even have believed it myself.

Until I saw her today.

A breeze blows in from Silver Lake and draws my eyes to the spot where it happened. Hidden just beyond the swell of sand dunes is a cluster of trees where Bree McTavish wrapped herself around me and stole my heart straight from my chest.

I've been trying to get it back ever since. Which either makes me a pathetic loser or … a pathetic loser. I groan and shake my head. I didn't come back here for the Long Ballers. I came back for *her*.

And fucking blew it the minute I saw her.

You're the best, Bree. God, did I really say that? And shit. A girlfriend? Right. I haven't had a serious girlfriend since high school, because I've been too hung up on her.

I panicked. Pure and simple. I went to the kitchen with a plan. I would casually greet her, gauge her reaction, and let things progress from there. But when she looked at me like I was the last person on Earth she wanted to see, it just slipped out. *Girlfriend.* Christ.

I left the kitchen, headed straight to the trash can, and dumped the food, appetite gone. Guilt can fill up an empty stomach faster than any meal when you have a mouth full of shame to chew on.

The door squeaks open behind me. A moment later, Grady appears and hands me another beer. "So, how is it?"

My shoulder, he means. I consider lying, but what's the point? Everyone knows the truth. The latest rankings show me in No Man's Land. Even if I get selected at the end of this month, it will be in a dreaded middle round where a player can linger for years in the minors before finally giving up. And forget about a signing bonus. I'm worth a tenth of my former self.

"Good as new," I finally say, giving the same answer I've been reciting for a month. At least it's true. They fixed the ligament.

"How many games did you miss?"

"First half of the season."

"They keep you behind the plate?"

I'm normally a catcher. "No. Coach moved me to third." Where the chances of having to throw hard and fast on a regular basis are lower. One of the most important measures of a catcher is his pop time—how fast he can make the relay to second base to break up a steal. You need a good shoulder on your throwing arm for that.

I couldn't have landed on my left side, could I?

"I'm sorry, man," Grady finally says. "It fucking sucks."

I snort and take a long pull on my beer. "Yeah, it does. You sure you're safe standing next to me?"

"I'll take my chances."

And that, in baseball world, is a true friend. I almost want to hug him.

"Want to sit out here and get drunk?" he asks.

"Hell, yes."

Grady drags over two wrought-iron chairs from a corner where they were stacked and stored for the winter. We sit down and prop our feet on the balustrade. Minutes stretch in silence.

Until a movement from under the terrace catches our eyes.

It's Bree, coming out of the side service entrance. A massive, overstuffed backpack weighs her down.

"Jesus, is she going camping or something?" Grady asks.

She walks to her car in the parking lot, unlocks it, opens the back door, and shoves the backpack inside. As she turns to get into the driver's seat, she looks up.

Even from this distance, I can feel the coldness in her gaze. I try to tell myself it's for the best. I don't have time to play this game anymore. I have too much at stake to get distracted even for a second. I should spend every minute I'm here playing for the scouts.

But when she climbs into her car and drives away, pain slices through me. Is this really it? Did my stupid rookie lie earlier officially kill this thing we pretend doesn't exist between us?

"Interesting rule you tacked on at the end of your speech in there," Grady says, opening his second beer.

"Should've been a rule all along. Might've saved me a lot of trouble."

His eyebrows shoot up again. "So, it's true about you guys?"

I whip my head to glare at him. "Is what true?"

"That you guys had a thing once."

"Is that what people say?"

Grady holds up his hands in a truce-like gesture. "I'm just saying what I've heard. And you don't exactly hide it, OK? You look at her like—"

"Like what?" I'm basically growling now.

"Like you have a thing. And you didn't exactly help matters with that little speech in there."

My fingers tighten around the bottle. "The guys can talk about me all they want. But they'd better keep their mouths shut about her."

"Yeah, I think you sent that message loud and clear. She's all yours."

Except she's not.

I turn my gaze to the empty parking spot where her car had been. And then my eyes drift back to the dunes and beyond, to that secluded place where I first felt what it was like to truly lose a piece of myself in a girl, the place where my mind still takes me when I'm asleep.

But that's where it needs to stay.

Secluded. In my dreams and in my past.

Because my real-life future is charging at me like a runner stealing home, and I'm still not sure what's going to be worse.

The falling down.

Or the getting up.

4

BREE

THE HOUSE IS silent and dark by the time I glide my bike up the sidewalk to the service door. It's after one o'clock in the morning. I should have been back two hours ago, but I didn't have much choice. The guys stayed up well beyond curfew, and Jax and Grady stayed on the terrace until almost twelve-thirty. I didn't factor that into my plans.

At this point, I'll get exactly four hours of sleep before I have to rise again, sneak in a shower in the old servants' quarters in the basement, slip out on my bike, retrieve my car from where I left it in the commuter lot by US-31, and return to start breakfast.

It has been my routine for three months.

It's still too cold at night to sleep in my car. I tried it in February when this whole mess began. By night two I knew it wasn't going to work. But it's too risky to leave my car at Edsel House overnight. I'd be busted within two days. The only thing that would be worse than being kicked out is the humiliation of being caught.

Darkness shields me as I slip my key into the lock of the service door beneath the terrace. Guilt gnaws at me for my deception. I feel like a thief, but the chill in the air chases away my reluctance. I quickly type in the security code on the panel on the wall inside and let the door shut quietly, holding onto the handle until the last second to make sure it doesn't slam and give me away. Thank God Mrs. Armitage and Matilda don't live here. If anything is going to give me away, it will be that damn dog.

A few steps takes me to the butler's pantry just past the back door. Once inside, I close the door and flip on the overhead light. My stuff is right where I left it, still a secret.

I change quickly into pajamas and pull the thin, frayed sleeping bag and pillow from my backpack. After I turn off the overhead light, I slip into my makeshift bed. Cold from the concrete floor seeps through. At least I'm inside. It only takes one night of not having a secure roof over your head to make you value even the shittiest of conditions.

I check to make sure my alarm clock is set and turned to the lowest possible volume.

Only then do I close my eyes and hope for sleep to chase away the memories that never want to leave me alone.

"When was the last time someone kissed you like they meant it?"

"N-never."

"That ends today."

Then his fingers wove into my hair and kissed me.

In our secluded circle of trees, with the lake breeze caressing our skin and the light of the moon illuminating us in romance, we made an oasis. Everything else disappeared but the feel of his gentle hands on my skin and the tender words he whispered. He erased the pain, the shame, the betrayal. After a lifetime of knowing I was nothing but a burden, he made me feel like a treasure. For a precious moment in time, I was wanted, needed, loved.

It was like a dream. A fantasy.

But when it was over, reality revealed the mirage for what it was. A shimmery illusion of useless desires that would only disappoint me in the end.

Keep my heart out of it? Too late. Jax Tanner stole it two years ago and never gave it back.

Damn fairy tales.

5

JAX

THE ALARM GOES off way too early. It's still dark out as I roll over with a muffled groan and reach for my phone with a heavy hand. My fingers brush the edge of it and send it crashing to the floor.

Fuuuuck. What the hell was I thinking with all that beer last night?

Temptation to ignore the annoying beep, beep, beep and roll back over nearly sucks me into submission. But no. I can't. I have to get in a run this morning before breakfast.

I stumble around my room, hating myself for getting drunk without unpacking my shit first. At least I get my own room and bathroom this year. Another perk of being a third-year player.

A wave of oh-shit-I'm-going-to-puke washes over me, and I brace my hands on the wall to suck in big gulps of air to chase it away. What the hell was I doing? My whole fucking career is on the line, and I sat out on that terrace last night getting drunk like a useless frat bro back at school with nothing better to do.

I force myself to pull on my running gear and remember at the last second to grab a hat. It might be June, but it's early June in northern Michigan. It's fucking freezing when I walk onto the terrace. My breath puffs around my face in crazy little clouds as I jog down the steps. My third year here, but I'm still not used to summer not being summer. I know it will be hot as balls by July, but Jesus. I blow on my hands and rub them together. Should've brought gloves, too.

I run through the shoulder and arm stretches my rehab doc taught me and then drop to the ground for a few quick warm-up push-ups.

A noise to my left draws my attention.

A creak.

Like the service door opening.

I stand up and blink in the dark. Bree slips outside with a furtive glance over her shoulder and that stuffed backpack weighing her down. She grabs a bike leaning against the stone wall, climbs on, and rides off.

What. The. Fuck.

I saw her leave last night. In her car. What the hell is she doing on a bike, leaving again?

I open my mouth to call out to her but stop myself. I can't do this. I don't have time to worry about her. I have my own fucking life to take care of.

But when I start running, my feet head in the same direction she went.

6

BREE

I MAKE it back by six.

I park my car in my normal spot, lock the backpack in the trunk, and head to the house. A pink glow from the sunrise casts just enough light to illuminate my fingers as I slip the key into the lock, but it's still dark inside as I type in the security code.

I walk into the kitchen. Flip on the lights.

And scream.

Jax stands in the center of the kitchen, guzzling water, sweat running down his face. He stares down at me over the rim of his bottle with a single eyebrow raised.

I clutch a hand to my heart and collapse against the wall. "What the hell, Jax? You scared the shit out of me!"

He finishes off the water and chucks the empty bottle into the recycling bin by the door. "What were you doing this morning?"

"What?"

"I saw you leave on a bike."

Oh shit. OhshitohshitohshitOHSHIT. He *saw* me. How could I have not planned for him or anyone else to see me in the morning? Of course, they get up early, especially this first week when they have long practices leading up to the start of games.

Well, that's that. I don't have a choice anymore. I can't wait until it fully warms up to start sleeping in my car. I'll just have to wear a lot of layers.

I mentally shake my head. It will be fine. I can sleep in the car. It's only for a few months. I've endured worse. It won't be colder than the January I spent alone in Brett's trailer with no heat, or the night he locked me out because I was late and I had to make do with just my coat on the porch.

"Bree?" he says, eyebrows raised.

I pull away from the wall. "I have to start breakfast."

"I tried to follow, but I lost sight of you."

"You tried to *follow* me? Are you stalking me?"

"What were you doing here so early? I saw you leave last night in your car."

"OK, you definitely sound like a stalker now. And you're not allowed in the kitchen," I say, trying to change the subject as I avoid his eyes. "Mrs. C is going to be here any minute."

My diversion tactics don't work. He takes two steps closer and crosses his arms over his chest. My eyes have a mind of their own, gaping at the bulging outlines of biceps and pecs beneath his long-sleeved running shirt.

I force myself to look at his face. His eyes are bloodshot, probably from his late night on the terrace.

A word appears out of nowhere. *Stormy.*

I now know exactly what is so different about him, what I couldn't articulate yesterday. Jax Tannner, for all his unending sexiness, has always been a puppy dog. Big eyes. Goofy grin. Gentle nature. If he had a tail, he'd wag it.

But this isn't a puppy in front of me. This is a full-grown alpha dog with a hot intensity that steals my breath. He was dangerous before, but now he's lethal, because all I want to do is lean. I want to rest my cheek on his chiseled chest and let the heat of his body envelop mine and chase away the chill of my night on the floor and my pre-dawn bike ride. I want to sink into his arms the way I did two summers ago.

But even if I could bring myself to do it—to live in the moment, as Lexi says—I can't. He has a girlfriend.

I try to walk around him but he widens his stance, blocking my way. "What's going on, Bree?"

"What's going on is that I need to heat the oven, because the cinnamon rolls aren't going to bake themselves."

"Are you in some kind of trouble?"

I go around the other side of him. "You jumped to that conclusion from me riding a bike?"

"Riding a bike at five o'clock in the morning after sneaking out with a backpack. Yeah. It's kind of suspicious."

"Oh, I get it," I snort, turning the dial on the oven. "You think I'm stealing."

"What? No! I would never think that."

I look over my shoulder. The wide-eyed shock of his expression suggests he's truly offended. Shame heats my cheeks as I walk to the fridge. "Breakfast won't be ready until seven, but I can make you something real quick, if you want."

He reaches out and stops me, fingers wrapped loosely around my wrist. A vein pops at his temple as if he's clenching his jaw. "I don't need you to serve me."

"It's my job."

"No, it's not. Your job is to cook for the entire team, not cater to me like Cinderella."

I snort again. "Really? What happened to *you're the best, Bree*?" I pull from his grasp. "And as you pointed out, I have to cook for the whole team, so can I please get on with it?"

The vein pops again. "I just want to make sure you're OK. Is that a crime?"

"I don't know. Why don't you check with your girlfriend?" I wince at the bitterness in my voice. How do you convince a guy you're not interested? Gripe sarcastically about his girlfriend. I hate me.

His lips part and then close twice until they press into a thin line like he's trying to hold in a confession. Weird. I see the same expression on my own face almost daily.

I point to the door. "Out. Please."

He lets out a long sigh and drags a weary hand across his beard. "Christ, Bree. Are we really going to do this again all summer?"

"No, we're not going to do *anything* this summer." I point to the door again. "So, please. You stay on your side of the door, and I'll stay on mine."

His lips nearly disappear. "Fine. You want me to stay on my side of the door? I'll do it. I'll walk out there and forget I ever met you, if that's what you want."

It's not.

"And believe me, my life would be a lot easier if I could, because I don't have time for this anymore."

Ouch.

"But you have to do something for me first."

"What?" I cross my arms to keep myself from touching my cheeks to see if the slap of his words left a mark.

"Tell me what the hell I did wrong."

I blink and stutter. "W-what?"

He steps closer, boxing me in between the heat of his body and the chill of the counter behind me. "I've spent two years torturing myself, wondering what I did to chase you away. So *please*. Just talk to me, and we can end this one and for all. What did I do?"

My tongue is thick and useless in my mouth. He's giving me the perfect chance to chase him off, to turn him away for good. I could say anything right now and end this cat-and-mouse game between us, once and for all. But I can't. It feels too good to stand in the circle of his heat and his strength. It would be so easy. I could fall into him, and something in his eyes tells me he would catch me.

But for how long?

I force my feet to back up, putting some much-needed breathing room between us. "I'm sorry you've been tortured for two years, and I'm sorry I ran away from you without an explanation. But it was just one night, and ..."

Something flickers in his eyes that looks a lot like hope. Which makes no sense. He has a girlfriend. "And what? Finish the sentence."

"And I was drunk. It meant nothing to me."

A thousand emotions flash across his face, each progressively more painful for me, until he settles on something hard and unreadable. Whatever distance I'd put between us, he eats up in one long step. His eyes are dark but vulnerable at the same time. "You know what pisses me off about that answer, Bree?"

My head shakes with tiny tremors of *no.*

"It's a lie."

Then without another word, he spins on his heel and crosses to the door. He slams his hands in the center, sending it swinging with a loud thud against the outer wall.

I jump and spin to lean on the prep counter for support. Part of me wants to race after him and apologize, tell him I was lying, that our night together meant more than it should. That I can't forget it. I can't forget him.

But this is for the best, right? This is the way it has to be.

So why am I shaking at the finality of it? Why am I lonely in this empty space where he stood? Why am I cold with the chill of his iciness? Why does the silence reverberate as loudly as his angry words?

"Was that Mr. Tanner I saw leaving the kitchen?"

I jump again, this time at the sound of Mrs. C's voice.

I turn away, trying to hide the wet shimmer in my eyes. "Ye-yes. He was wondering if we had any, um, bottles of water."

"Turn around," Mrs. C orders.

I cringe but do what she tells me, because there's no disobeying that tone of voice. She may look like Mrs. Potts from *Beauty and the Beast*, but when she uses that tone, you're in for a talking-to. I try not to visibly wince as I meet her gaze. She stands with her arms crossed and brow furrowed.

"What happened?"

"Nothing."

A silver eyebrow arches over a skeptical stare. "Honey, do you think I'm blind? You and that boy have been circling each other like hungry cats since he started on this team. I've always liked him, but I swear to God, if he hurt you, I will kill him with one of my own frying pans."

I'm so shocked by her sudden display of, well, *caring* that all I can do is laugh. It's a sad, pathetic, watery laugh, but it's still a laugh. I swipe my hand over my eyes. "He didn't hurt me. I think ... "

My voice trails off as painful realization settles with a thud in my stomach. *I think I hurt him.*

I turn away from Mrs. C again in case I'm not as good as I hope I am at hiding my emotions. But then I suck in a breath and shove everything that hurts way down inside where it belongs. Out of sight. Out of the way.

I clear my throat and turn back around. "The oven is pre-heating for the cinnamon rolls."

Mrs. C nods. "Good. Let's get to work. Because we have a lot of work to do."

Right. Not the least of which is figuring out how and where to sleep in my car tonight.

The last thing I need is to fall apart over Jax Tanner again.

The closet was nice while it lasted, but Jax?

He was never mine to begin with.

7

JAX

"TANNER!"

The bark of my name draws me up short as I wait for my turn in the batting cage. I turn to see Coach Bill Abrams saunter out of the dugout, a wad of sunflower seeds bulging out of his left cheek. He hacks a shell from his mouth and wipes away the spittle that sticks to his unshaven chin.

"Drop that fucking wood and get your ass over here," he growls.

What the hell? Practice started exactly three minutes ago, and I'm already getting my ass handed to me? Then again, why not? A good go-around with my coach might give me something else to focus on then the soul-sucking replay of my fight with Bree. I don't know what was worse: the lie she tried to feed me, or how badly I want to go back and get the truth out of her.

Either way, I'll take anything—even a tirade by Coach—to justify my bad mood.

I kick the dirt from my cleats with the top of my bat and try to act like I'm not secretly shitting my pants. "What's up, Coach?"

"I told you to drop the fucking stick."

I glance around. Everyone is watching but pretending not to. I nod at the wide-eyed bat boy—some local Little Leaguer who has probably been waiting years to get the chance to volunteer for the Sluggers. He looks like he regrets it now as he runs over and takes the bat from me.

Coach waits for me along the third base line, arms crossed and eyes glowering over his puffy cheeks.

"What's up," I ask, getting closer.

"You trying to get me blacklisted, son?"

"Um, no, sir…"

"You think I'm ever going to get another top prospect sent to my team if I let you fuck up your shoulder again?"

"I'm not a top prospect anymore."

"Did I tell you to speak?"

I look around again. The guys aren't even pretending anymore. Everything on the field has stopped to watch the action in the warning track.

"We need to take it easy with you for a couple of days until I hear from your docs, but there you are, almost no warm-up." He gestures like he's jerking off. "Yanking on that stick like it's your goddamned pecker."

Don't laugh. Do not laugh. I cough and look down. "I warmed up, Coach. It's good—"

"No hitting. Not until I've had time to build a training program. Until then." He points at the outfield where relievers and closers nervously bounce the balls in their gloves.

I blink as his intentions become clear. "You're shitting me."

He spits out another shell. "Nope."

"You want me to catch bullpen?" Of all the menial-assed tasks on the roster, that's about as low as it gets.

He sticks a fat finger in my face. "Hey, asshole. Watch your fucking mouth. There are kids around here." He spits again. "And if you have somewhere else you'd rather be, I have a hundred guys on a waiting list who'd give their left nut to take your place."

He's right. I'm being an asshole. But, fuck. The bullpen? "Sorry, Coach," I mumble.

He tilts his head and scratches his whisker-covered jowls. "Look, son. You got a raw deal. I know that. Everyone knows it. But you're moping around here like your entire career is already over."

I bite back a bunch of words that would earn me a permanent spot on his shit list. He doesn't understand. Coach Abrams was never a real prospect. He was drafted after college in the thirty-eighth of forty rounds and spent six years bouncing between minor league teams without a prayer of playing a single inning in the bigs. He doesn't know what it's like to spend your entire life knowing you were born to go all the way, only to have it taken away in a split-second slip on the ice.

Coach lets out a long sigh. "I've debated all morning about whether to tell you this or not, but I guess there's no reason not to."

I snap my gaze back to his, because this doesn't sound good. "What?"

"I got a call from the Midwest scout for the Rays last night."

"The Tampa Bay Rays?"

"No, the Bum Fuck Egypt Rays," Coach snorts. "Yes, the Tampa Bay Rays, dumbshit."

"What'd he want?"

"They're coming to look at you next week."

Whatever is left of breakfast in my stomach lurches toward my throat. "For what round?"

Coach shrugs and dodges my gaze. "You know they don't decide that stuff this early."

The hell they don't. "What fucking round?"

Coach sighs again. "Somewhere in the high teens, I think. Or, you know, maybe low twenties."

I stumble backward. Low twenties. No Man's Land. Holy fuck. It's really happening. A sour taste stings the back of my throat.

"It's not the end of the world, Tanner."

Except, it is. It's the end of my world—the world I knew, the world I've built for myself, the world I promised to my family to make up for everything they've put up with and done for me so I could have this dream. I plant my hands on my head and turn around aimlessly. My eyes scour the diamond, my teammates, my whole goddamned life.

"Son, look at me."

I swallow against the rising revolution in my gut and obey him. He has that stern glower on his face again. Deep grooves line his forehead. "It's a cruel game we play, Tanner. It's cruel what we do to kids like you. Build them up all their lives to think something's a sure thing only to yank it away from them."

I wonder if we're still talking about me.

"But I've been doing this a long time," he says. "And I only really know one fucking thing. Life doesn't give a shit about our game plans. And the only mark of a real prospect is how he reacts to the curve ball he never saw coming." Coach bends until his face is inches from mine. "So, you need to decide right now how you want to do this. You can either swing with all your might and knock that fucker out of the park, or you can whine at the umpire for a bad strike call. It's your choice."

He straightens and spits again with a nod toward the bullpen. "Now gear up and give me your best, or get the fuck off my team."

My legs are rubber as I walk to the dugout to grab my catcher's gear. I pull each piece on by rote. Helmet. Mask. Shin pads. Chest guard. It's the uniform of my life, but right now it feels foreign on my body. Like it's no longer mine.

Everyone gives me a wide berth as I lumber toward the bullpen, because this shit is contagious. I crouch down sixty feet from one of the relief pitchers who looks around like he's trying to gauge whether my bad luck is an airborne pollutant.

"Just throw the fucking ball," I yell. He gives me a poor excuse for a heater that lands with a weak thud in my mitt.

I stand and lob it back just as weakly, because a terrifying thought has taken root in my brain.

What if I throw out my shoulder for good?

What if I never get drafted at all?

What the fuck do I have without baseball?

I crouch again, on the verge of a violent puke.

Not because of the questions.

But because of the answer.

Nothing.

I have nothing.

I am nothing.

8

BREE

IT'S A LIE.

All day, those three words have played on a constant repeat in my head. Not because of the tone in which they were delivered or the hurt that simmered underneath. I can't get them out of my head because I can't stop wondering how he knew.

"Wake up, girl. It's gettin' limp."

I blink out of my trance as Mrs. C pokes my shoulder. I look down at the asparagus and curse the telltale greening of the stalks. I shut off the fire and move the skillet.

Asparagus is serious business in Mrs. C's kitchen. This part of Michigan is one of the nation's leading producers of the stuff, and you don't get to work the major meals in Mrs. C's kitchen until you've mastered it.

It's not like a penis, Mrs. C proclaimed one day. *The longer you mess around with it, the softer it gets.*

Then she cackled at my red face. I didn't have a lot of experience with penises—hard or soft—at that point and, frankly, still don't. But thanks to her, I'm terrified that the next time I sleep with a guy all I'm going to think about is whether he's getting too green down there.

Jax's asparagus was perfect, I'm pretty sure.

I mentally smack myself. I grab the thankfully still-crisp stalks with a pair of tongs and set them on the cutting board next to the stove. They're the topping to my warm spinach salad that will serve as tonight's first course.

"I'll help," Lexi says, siding up next to me at the counter.

I smile in thanks. We work in an assembly line for a few minutes, just like we used to do when I lived with her and her mom in high school after my teacher discovered the truth about my living conditions—that Brett had taken off for Florida to work a winter farm down there and left me behind. Alone.

Cooking was a family affair In Lexi's house. After making dinner together, the three of us would gather around their worn dining table to eat and laugh and talk about the crazy shit that happened at school or in the hair salon. That's when I knew I wanted to be a chef. Living with them made me love food, because it made me realize food is love.

Lexi suddenly looks over. "You know, this would be a decent recipe to enter in the contest."

I shrug. "Still thinking about it."

"No, you're not. You're just delaying until you purposely miss the deadline."

I hide my expression as I move several salads to a tray. I nod at one of the teen girls hovering nearby who is helping tonight. She lifts it and carries it out to the dining room.

"It's the money, isn't it?" Lexi asks quietly.

I don't answer as I start filling another tray with salad bowls.

"My mom will help you out. You know she will."

"Your mom has already done enough for me."

A second teenager takes the next tray.

"I swear, Bree. I'll never understand your concept of what it means to do *enough* for someone you care about," Lexi says.

"It means there's a fine line between accepting help and being a burden."

"That's ridiculous—"

I hold up my hand to cut her off. After what happened with Jax this morning, I'm one step away from Kardashian Cry Face, and a fight with Lexi isn't going to help.

"I'm not asking your mom for money, Lexi." I slide the last salad onto the last tray. "And forget about the contest. It's not going to happen."

I ignore the waiting teenager and instead pick up the tray myself. I back out the swinging door and turn around to scan which table is still waiting for salad.

It takes a moment for my eyes to adjust to the dim lighting. Mrs. Armitage tends to go overboard on ambiance for these dinners. Votive candles flicker on every table, casting yellow shadows against the faces of the players and along the mahogany wood panels that line the walls. It's like she wants to remind everyone of her Gilded Age ancestry. Her great-great-grandfather was some big lumber baron who built the house as a hunting club for his cronies, probably so they could stand around with cigars and laugh about screwing over the little guys on their way to being kings of the world.

I scan the tables again.

And stop on the one where Jax sits. Because *of course* his table would be the one still waiting.

He looks up, and our eyes collide. My heart takes off. He's sort of dressed up—as much as these guys dress up, anyway—in dark jeans and a checkered shirt that looks like he pulled it fresh from a J.Crew bag just today. His hair is wet, as if he emerged from the shower no more than ten minutes ago.

I head toward his table just as he stands, that vein popping along his forehead once again. He meets me halfway and reaches for the tray.

"What are you doing?" I hiss.

"Helping."

"Sit down before Mrs. Armitage notices."

"You don't have to serve people, Bree."

"It's. My. Job."

In my vehemence, the tray wobbles. He reaches under it to steady it, and his fingers brush mine. A shockwave races up my arm. An unmistakable flare of his nostrils tells me he felt it, too, and for a moment, we're locked into a surprised staring contest. We're supposed to be done, aren't we? He's supposed to be forgetting he ever met me.

But that's not what I see in his eyes right now.

Coach Abrams' voice breaks the spell. "What the hell are you doing, Tanner? Either help or leave her alone."

Great. Just great. The guys are now watching, and Jax, being the Prince Charming that he is, just stands tall and takes the tray from me. "I got it," he says firmly.

Then he turns away, tray in hand, taking his teammates' shit-talking in stride.

I trudge back through the swinging door to the kitchen. Mrs. C looks up, brow furrowed. "Did you forget the tray?"

"One of the guys took it to help."

"Mr. Tanner, I assume."

I toss up my hands. "What do you want me to do? Throw bacon at him?"

She manages a small quirk of a smile and nods at a massive pot cooling on the front of the stove. "Fine. You can help me finish the mashed potatoes." She looks at Lexi. "Go fetch that last tray, will you?"

I avoid Lexi's probing gaze as she walks past to do Mrs. C's bidding. She's pissed at me about the contest. She doesn't understand, and I have no idea how to make her. Despite growing up without a father and being subjected to the town's cruel gossip, Lexi has no idea what it feels like to spend your entire life as someone's problem to deal with. She grew up in a home with unending love and generosity.

Love in her world never came with a ticking clock.

Dinner passes blissfully fast after that. The routine of the kitchen takes over until I'm focused only on the pride of producing something good, something that will fill people up with warmth and flavor.

When everyone finally clears out, and it's just me in the kitchen, I turn myself over to my favorite reward for a long day— visions of my own kitchen to run. My own restaurant.

A place I will build with my own two hands and hard work.

A place no one can take away.

A place where I can *live in the moment* whenever I want.

Most importantly, a place with no pesky dogs determined to ruin me.

My subconscious adds the last part abstractly, and it takes the rest of my brain a second to catch up to why. I'm bent over the prep counter giving it a last scrub down when I see the ball of white race past me toward the open door of the pantry.

I suck in a gasp and drop the cloth in my hand.

Jax comes up behind me with a mumbled apology about returning a dish from his room and accidentally letting her in. I barely hear him, because I'm trapped in the nightmare again. My feet are stuck in molasses, my senses in slow motion.

I take off after her. "Matilda, no!"

She doesn't listen. If anything, her little legs scamper faster.

She disappears into the pantry like a hound chasing a fox.

Except in this game, I'm the prey.

9

JAX

I KNOW Matilda isn't supposed to be in the kitchen, but Bree's reaction is over the top. Her face pinches with panic as she takes off after the dog into the massive walk-in pantry on the other side of the kitchen.

My brain tells me to set the dish down, turn around, and return to my *side of the door* like I promised this morning. To pretend I didn't use this stupid plate as a lame excuse for seeing her because my body is still buzzing from the way it felt to touch her, even just that tiny brush of her finger against mine. To ignore the flare of desire that burned in her eyes and confirmed my suspicions that her story this morning was a lie.

But my brain is never in charge when I'm around her. So instead of walking away, I follow.

Bree is on her knees in the corner, fighting with the dog over that bra again.

"What are you doing?"

Bree whips her gaze over her shoulder. "Shut the door!"

"Why?"

"So, she can't escape!"

I do what she asks and return to her side. My laugh dies in my throat as my eyes take in the entire scene. A large duffel bag is tipped over, spilling a collection of clothes and bathroom shit and hair stuff.

My stomach churns. "Bree, what the hell is going on?"

Her hands slip, and Matilda takes a leap over Bree's legs with the bra in her mouth. Bree curses and whips around as if to give chase again. I drop to my knees and grab her hands.

"Stop!" I say, harsher than I intended, but fuck, I'm suddenly shaking inside and out, because this all adds up to something I don't like.

Sneaking out this morning on a bike.

Returning with her car.

All this stuff.

Her panic.

"Why do you have all this stuff here?"

Bree groans and squeezes her eyes shut. "Just go, Jax."

"Oh shit," I breathe, rocking back on the balls of my feet. "What the fuck? Are you *sleeping* in here?"

Bree yanks her hands from my grip. "It doesn't matter. Just help me clean it up before Mrs. Armitage comes looking for Matilda and finds all this."

Bree frantically starts shoving items back in her bag. I blink out of my stupor and help, but I'm too shocked and slow to do much more than get in her way.

"Bree, you have to talk to me. Why don't you want Mrs. Armitage to see this?"

"Because she'll fire me on the spot!" Bree fights to close the zipper on the bag and then stands, hoisting the strap over her shoulder. The damn thing nearly sends her toppling into the wall.

"Christ," I mutter, rising. "Give me that."

She jerks away from me. "You want to help? Get my stupid bra away from the dog."

I follow her point just in time to see Matilda dart behind a shelving unit. "No. Forget about the bra and tell me what the hell is going on!"

Bree lets out a frustrated growl and stomps around me. I use my long legs to my full advantage to cross in front of her and block her path. "Where are you going?"

"I'm leaving."

"Leaving where?"

Her lips part, and that split-second hesitation tells me everything I don't want to know. "You don't have anywhere to go, do you?"

Her throat works against a hard swallow. "It's just temporary."

My jaw clenches. "How long have you been sleeping in here?"

"Jax—"

"How. Long."

"Three months."

All the air in my lungs escapes. "You've been sleeping in this closet for three months?"

She gets that thin-lipped defensive look on her face that I'm starting to recognize as her weapon of choice.

"This is really none of your business," she snaps.

I drag my hands through my hair and stare at the floor. She's right. It's none of my business. Not really. But *she* is. All that bull-shit I said this morning about being done and forgetting I ever met her. It was just that—bullshit. I let my hands fall away and look up again. "Start at the beginning."

She stares at me as an internal debate plays out on her face. She doesn't know if she can trust me, and that realization hurts more than anything else that has happened between us. "Bree, have I ever given you any reason to think I would hurt you?"

"N-no."

"Then tell me what happened."

She swallows. "It was just going to be until summer ended, or at least until it warmed up enough to sleep in my car."

"Your car?"

"Do you want to hear this, or not?"

I press my lips together and nod.

"I had an apartment. But my car died in February, and it was going to cost more to fix it than it was worth. I can't *not* have a car, not in the winter, not with the wedding gigs I've been picking up. So, I had to buy a new one, and that meant digging into the money I've been saving for culinary classes in Lansing. My apartment lease was almost up anyway, so ..." She shrugs. "It just made sense."

"It made *sense*? To essentially be homeless?"

"I don't expect you to understand."

"But what about family? I thought your stepdad lived here."

"No, he, uh... He moved to Florida."

"Lexi's family, then!"

Her eyes shift away. "Like I said. I don't expect you to under-stand. And it's only temporary. At the end of August, I'll move into an apartment in Lansing and—" She shuts up with a gasp at the sound of the swinging door in the kitchen.

Someone's coming.

"Oh shit," she breathes.

I press my finger to her lips.

"Matilda? Here princess. Where are you?"

Bree's eyes bug out of her face as Matilda races from her hiding spot with a loud bark to answer her owner.

"Matilda?" Mrs. Armitage calls again, louder and closer than before.

I act without thinking. I grab Bree by the arm and haul her behind the massive shelving unit where she hid her stuff before. I press her body against the wall and shield it with mine. Her bag falls from her shoulder and lands with a loud thump.

We both freeze.

Bree's breath locks in her throat.

I lean down until my lips cover her ear. "Breathe," I whisper.

Her head shakes. Her body trembles. She's good and truly terrified of being caught, and I'm starting to understand why. She doesn't just need this job. She *needs* this job.

Instinct takes over, and I wrap arms around her. She tucks against me willingly and lets me cup the back of her head. A sensation of falling sends my stomach to my shoes because, holy fuck, she's in my arms.

Finally.

This was never how I imagined it happening again, but I'll take what I can get.

Matilda barks again, and we hear the pantry door creak open. "Oh, my poor, poor baby. How did you get shut in here?" Mrs. Armitage croons.

The dog's nails scrape on the concrete floor as she runs out of the pantry.

Mrs. Armitage doesn't follow, though.

She fucking walks in.

"Oh, who left this light on again?" the old woman mutters.

"Going to have to talk to Mrs. Caruthers about these kids she hires."

The room suddenly goes black.

Seconds later, the door closes. Mrs. Armitage's voice grows more and more faint until the pantry is silent once again.

Bree sinks into my chest. "Oh my God."

"Well, that solves that mystery," I say against her hair.

"What mystery?"

"The C stands for Caruthers."

Bree snorts against my shoulder, but then she stiffens in my arms.

"Jax," she whispers.

"Yeah?" My voice barely works.

Her breathing kicks up again, faster, shallower. We're wrapped in total darkness, but I don't need to see to glide my hands up her back. I don't need my eyes to help my hands find their way to her cheeks. I don't need light to guide me as I tilt her head back, dip mine, and lower my mouth to hover over hers.

Bree makes a noise.

And wrenches away.

10

BREE

OH MY GOD. What am I doing? One minute ago, I was on the verge of being caught by Mrs. Armitage, and now I'm clinging to Jax like he's a tree I want to climb.

Jax's fingers tighten against my cheeks. "Bree."

"I have to go." I pull away from his touch, from his body, from his desire. It's so dark in the pantry that I nearly trip over my duffel bag.

Jax's fingers wrap around my bicep to hold me steady. "Where?"

I bend to find the strap of my bag and yank it over my shoulder. Jax lets go of my arm as I stumble toward the pantry door.

"Bree, wait." Jax's footsteps pound behind me as I start to leave.

"I can't. That was too close."

"What was? Almost getting caught or almost kissing me?"

I grab the door handle and turn it. I can't answer him because I'm not sure of the answer.

Jax's hand covers mine and stops me. "Just wait a minute. Where the hell are you planning to go?"

"I'll figure it out."

"What does that mean?"

"I'll sleep in my car."

"Your car?!" His voice cracks with an incredulous squawk. "There's a thunderstorm coming!"

"I have blankets."

"No. You're not sleeping in your car."

I shove his hand away and turn the handle. "I've done it before."

I push open the door and storm into the kitchen. My bag bangs against my back and my shoulders. Jax follows, his footsteps clipped and angry.

My bag slips from my shoulder as I yank open the service door.

Jax grabs it. "Dammit, give me that."

I let him slide it off my arm, but I don't turn around. And I don't stop. Because I know he'll follow. An involuntary shiver races up my spine as I step into the cool night. The storm is close. I can feel it in the air. Everything crackles, and the waves on the beach crash with unusual power.

I duck out from under the portico that covers the service entrance just as a crack of thunder breaks the silence of the night.

Jax grabs my arm again. "Bree, please. Just stop. *Please.*"

He turns me around, and a flash of lightning across the sky illuminates an expression on his face I can only describe as desperate. "You can stay in my room."

"You're crazy."

"I'll sleep on the floor."

"No. It's too risky." Not because I could get fired for it, but because my heart would lose all perspective to be that close to him for a whole night. I was pressed against him for a mere thirty seconds in the closet and look what happened there.

"No one will know. I have the corner suite. I can take you up the back stairs and sneak you in that way."

I look over my shoulder at my car. He has no idea what he's offering me. He might as well dangle the whole fucking world in front of my face.

I look at him. "Jax, I can't—"

"Dammit, Bree!" He suddenly yells. "Why are you being so stubborn?"

I snap. "Why the hell do you care?"

He stumbles backward, and I realize with a jolt I've never seen him look like this. Storm cells rolling in from Lake Michigan have less intensity than the one raging in his eyes.

He drops my bag and surges forward. "How can you even ask that?"

"Because you have a girlfriend! Remember?"

His face falls until the hard edge in his eyes morphs into a soft regret. He drags his hands through his hair and looks somewhere over my shoulder. "No, I don't."

My heart coughs. "Excuse me?"

"I don't have a girlfriend. I lied."

I try to respond, but I can't. A weird fluttering in my chest sends my breathing into overdrive. He doesn't have a girlfriend. I don't know if I'm relieved or scared shitless. Without a girlfriend between us, what excuse can I use this year as a crutch for holding him at arm's length?

"*Why?*" I breathe.

"I don't know. You were staring at me like I was an invasive species, and fuck, I don't know. Maybe I wanted to see your reaction."

A cold drop of rain splashes my cheek. "You-you wanted to make me jealous?"

"I don't know." His face hardens again. "But you lied to me, too."

"Of course, I lied! You really think that night meant nothing to me? It meant everything to me!"

"Then why?" he cries, wrapping his hands around my arms. "Why did you run away? Why do you keep pushing me away?"

"Because you're a prospect!" I blurt, angry and thick-voiced.

"*What?*"

"You're him," I shout. "The one they warn us about when we're growing up here. The one who has all the looks and all the smiles. The one with big promises who can charm the pants off any girl they want."

He can barely contain his fury as he sputters a response. "Charm the pants off …? Is that what you think I was doing that night? That I'm trying to do now? You think you're just some ball bunny I'm trying to score with?"

"No."

"Then what the hell did you mean?"

"You're a *prospect*," I say again, as if emphasizing the word will somehow make it mean more this time. "And there just aren't a lot of prospects for a girl like me. Not with a guy like you."

"Well, this is your lucky day, Bree," he breathes, voice a low rumble as he closes the distance between us again. "Because I'm not much of a *prospect* anymore."

Then he grips the back of my head.

And kisses me.

My body reacts instinctively, like a cannonball leap into a cold lake. I stiffen and suck in a gasp at the shock of it, the surprise of it, the giddy recklessness of it.

But in the next instant, as his fingers relax and weave into my hair, as his mouth softens against mine with a low moan, and as his other hand finds a home on the small of my back, I start to sink. Memory and longing drag me under.

A murky voice in the back of my mind tries to throw me a line and yells at me to grab on because it's only going to hurt in the end, that I'm just feeling vulnerable and needy right now, that even if I manage to crest the surface again, I'm going to end up coughing and sputtering on the beach.

For two years, I've been kicking against this current, barely keeping my head above the crashing waves of my want for him. But now I'm drowning all over again, helpless in his rogue wave. And all I can do is swim to him.

Thunder cracks overhead with another flash of light. Jax pulls me closer until my body is flush against his, and I rise on tiptoe to wrap my arms around his neck. Rain pelts our bodies and soaks our clothes.

I don't know which one of us takes the kiss deeper, but suddenly we're open-mouthed and greedy. My hands dive into his thick, rain-soaked hair. A guttural noise rumbles in his chest, and he spins us both to press me against the stone wall under the portico. I gasp again, not from the shock of the cold stone but from the burn of the heat between us.

Jax braces his hands on either side of me and leans, plundering my mouth, scrambling my senses. His beard scrapes my skin. My fingernails scrape his scalp.

When he abandons my mouth to nip and kiss a trail down my

jaw, I answer with a moan and a tilt of my head. I feel drunk. Alive. Dizzy. I feel like I did that night, when he held out his hand and tugged me close and asked me if I wanted to take a walk.

I want to experience it all again—the swirling whirlpool of desire. The slide of his skin on mine. The thick pressure of him pushing inside me. The aching pleasure of my body welcoming him.

Jax claims my mouth again and wedges a thick, powerful thigh between both of mine. He rocks into me, and I press back. We're groaning together, sliding against each other. I shove my hands inside his shirt and draw his groan of pleasure in my open mouth.

"Bree," he pants against my lips. "God, Bree. You taste so fucking good."

He kisses me again. He slides a hand down my left side and hoists my leg over his hip. A sound bursts from my throat—a cross between a sob and moan—as I grind against him. He feels so good. This is crazy, but I can't stop. I don't want to.

But suddenly he does.

He wrenches his lips away and whips around, hands on his head. "Fuck. Fuck!"

I slump against the wall. What the... Oh my God. What am I doing?

Jax turns around, out of breath, an apology on his face. He opens his mouth but then shuts it before squeezing the back of his neck and dropping his gaze. After a moment, his hand falls away. "I'm sorry. Christ, Bree, I'm sorry."

"For kissing me?"

"For not asking permission."

"I wasn't exactly a passive participant."

He puffs out a sad laugh and squeezes his neck again.

I pull away from the wall. "I should go."

"No." He closes the distance between us again. He slides his hand along the curve of my jaw, gentle and rough at the same time. His voice tugs at my chest with a single, final plea. "*Stay.*"

JAX

I'M SHAKING.

I've never lost control like that before—not even that night two years ago. Now she's staring at me with a mixture of confusion and fear, and I can't fucking blame her. I pawed at her like a drunken frat boy. My breath catches in my chest as I watch the indecision play out on her face.

Finally, after what feels like an entire inning, she nods. "OK."

I grab her things and take her hand. We try to soften our footsteps as we head up the back stairs. At the top, I peek around the corner to make sure the hallway is clear, and then I lead her to my room.

It's dark inside, but the blinds are open. Lightning flashes as I shut and lock the door, and for a moment, I freeze.

She's really here.

In my room.

Standing before me and breathing heavy.

I want time to stand still so I can memorize how she looks in this moment with her hair wet and skin glistening. But then I remember why she's really here, and it's not to be mauled by me.

I clear my throat. "You can, um, change in the bathroom, if you want. There are towels in there."

She looks down at her clothes and then to her bag. Both are soaked. "I don't think I have anything to change into."

An image of her wet, naked body flashes through my mind.

I turn around to open a drawer in my dresser. I grab a t-shirt and a pair of basketball stores.

"Here," I say, turning again. "They'll be too big, obviously. But you can sleep in them."

She takes them from me with a nod and a quiet *thank you*. Then she grabs that massive duffel bag and walks into the private bathroom I've never been happier to have. The door closes with a soft click. I immediately bend to plant my hands on my knees. What the hell am I doing?

I listen to the sounds of her getting ready for bed. The zip of her bag. The splash of water in the sink. The muffled flush of the toilet. A moment later, the door opens. She steps out, face painted with a nervous expression. Her wet clothes are balled in her hands. "I wasn't sure what to do with these."

My mouth won't work at first, because I can't stop staring. My t-shirt hangs all the way to her thighs, but she's not wearing the shorts.

"They kept falling off," she whispers.

I nod. At least I think I nod. I'm not really sure what's happening with my muscles right now. "Right," I manage to say. "Um, do you want to hang your wet clothes over the shower curtain?"

"S-sure."

She turns back around, and I watch from the doorway as she rises on tiptoe to fling her wet t-shirt and shorts over the metal bar. My mind immediately wonders where her bra is, but I shake away the question. I'm trying to talk myself out of my raging hard-on, not make it worse.

She turns back around, hands tugging at the hem of the shirt.

"I, uh, I need to change," I say.

She skirts past me with what sounds like an apology of some sort. I grab a clean t-shirt and shorts for myself and then close myself in the bathroom. Her toothbrush lies on the counter of the sink, still wet. A pink comb is next to it. Something warm spreads through my chest because something feels right about her stuff being in my bathroom.

I change quickly, brush my teeth, and open the door. She's sitting on the edge of the mattress but jumps up when I walk out as if I'd be mad.

I dump my wet clothes in a clothes basket next to the bathroom door and then face her, hands on my hips. "You can have the bed. I'll sleep on the floor."

"It's your bed. I can take the floor."

"You've been sleeping on a floor for three months."

"Jax—"

"Take the bed, Bree."

I hold in a groan as she turns around and crawls on top of the blanket. The shirt rises to reveal two perfectly rounded butt cheeks peeking out from the bottom of her underwear.

She slips under the covers, sitting awkwardly. "What are you going to sleep on?"

I open my closet door and yank down the extra blanket and

pillow that were here when I arrived. "This," I say, turning back around.

I drop the pillow to the floor and shake the blanket to unfold it. She watches me, hands clutching my plain, navy comforter over her lap.

"Jax."

I look up.

"Thank you for this."

"You don't have to keep thanking me."

"Yes, I do."

Annoyance floods my veins and finally finishes off the wood in my pants. I don't want her to be grateful, like I'm doing a good-deed for a stranger. I lower myself to the floor, twist the pillow to plump it up, and then lay on my back, drawing the thin blanket over me at the same time.

I hear the slide of her skin against sheets. If I make it through this night without a raging wet dream, I'll deserve a goddamned medal.

I roll on my side, away from her.

Minutes later, I roll back the other way.

A few minutes after that, I flop onto my back.

"Are you OK?" Her voice is soft.

"Fine."

"You keep rolling over."

"I can't get to sleep."

"Do you want—"

"Don't ask me if I want the bed."

She gets quiet. But not for long. "Jax?"

"Yeah?"

"What did you mean before, about not being a prospect anymore?"

I don't answer right away, and she obviously gets the wrong idea. "You don't have to tell me."

There it is again. She's putting distance between us, as if we're strangers. "I hurt my shoulder," I say, edgy. "I had to have surgery."

"When?"

"Last winter."

"I'm sorry. I didn't know."

She's just rubbing it in now. She obviously doesn't stalk my social media accounts like I do hers.

"Are you OK now?" she asks.

"Good as new."

"Then why aren't you a prospect anymore?"

"Because I'm damaged goods."

She's quiet for a second. Then, "That's a horrible thing to say about yourself."

"That's baseball."

"So, what does that mean?"

"It means that if I get drafted this year, I probably won't get a great offer."

"But you still have a year left of school."

"I'm twenty-one and just finished my junior year. I'm eligible."

"But couldn't you just finish school and try again next year?"

"It's not that simple. If I refuse to sign with a team this year and go back to school, I might not get drafted again. Which would make me a free agent. And the chances of getting signed after that are dicey, at best."

"How is that fair?" Her voice squeaks higher, and I hear the sheets shift. I look up. She stares down at me with a look of righteous indignation that makes my heart kick up a notch. She cares more than she wants me to believe. If our kiss didn't convince me before, her gaze does now.

"What if you don't want to be drafted this year?" she whispers fiercely. "How can they just force you to?"

"They can't. The choice is always mine whether I want to sign with a team or not."

"But if you don't sign, you risk losing it all!"

"Pretty much, yeah."

"That's not fair!"

"That's baseball," I say again.

She suddenly gasps. "Wait. You can't sleep on the floor! Your shoulder!"

"I'm fine, Bree."

"No. I'll take the floor. This is stupid."

"No."

"It's *your* room."

"Yeah, so I get to say who sleeps where."

We stare at each other, a battle of wills.

She breaks first and lets out a small sigh. "Just get up here. I'm sure we can survive sleeping in the same bed, Jax."

My whole body goes stiff. As in, my whole body. So, yeah, maybe not about the whole surviving in the same bed thing.

"Jax?"

"Are you sure?"

"Yes."

I stand up and watch as she scoots close to the wall. The movement stretches my t-shirt across her breasts. OK. Wow. This is going to be difficult, because I want to eat her alive.

I peel back the comforter and slide in next to her. The bed is warm from her body, the pillow damp from her hair.

She lays on her side, and her arm brushes mine as she curls it under her head. I roll my head to look at her. "You OK?"

She smiles. "Yeah. You?"

I nod. If I say *yes*, I'll be lying, because I'm *not* OK. This is going to be the longest fucking night of my life.

"Thank you—"

"Stop thanking me."

"OK."

We stare at each other. She's so close that I can smell whatever lotion lingers on her skin.

"I'm sorry about your shoulder," she says.

"It happens." My voice sounds like I've taken up smoking.

"But you've worked your whole life for this. If I got that close to opening my own restaurant and then something happened that wasn't even my own fault, I'd be pretty pissed."

"Is that what you want? Your own restaurant?"

Her smile grows. "Yeah. Someday."

I roll onto my side to face her. "What kind of restaurant?"

Her eyes get a faraway look. "Something accessible but high-end. With a focus on seasonal, locally grown products from sustainable farms." She meets my eyes. "Something wholesome and fresh. Totally farm-to-table."

Her voice is faint over the roar in my ears. Right now, with that look on her face and that excited lilt in her voice, she's my Bree from the beach.

"Sounds incredible," I finally say. "I have no idea what most of that means, but it sounds awesome."

Her laugh makes my stomach take flight.

"I want to use local, environmentally friendly farms for my ingredients. Not big corporate farms or big slaughter houses. Like,

I want to be able to get cherries from a local farm in the morning and feed them to customers that night."

She sighs, and her eyes dim a little. "But that's a long time away. I have to get my associate's degree, and then try to get into an advanced culinary program, and then pay my dues working for other chefs first. I need to work overtime this summer to move to Lansing and get started."

"And that's why you're trying to save money."

She rolls onto her back and stares at the ceiling. "Yep. Every penny counts."

"What if you couldn't have a restaurant?"

"Then I'd write cookbooks, or work as a head chef somewhere or," she shrugs, "I don't know. There are a lot of things I could do."

I envy her. Not her current circumstances, but her confidence in the future and in herself. I used to know what that felt like.

"What about you? If you can't play baseball, I mean."

"I have no idea." I thought I'd feel like a total loser admitting that out loud, but I don't. Maybe it feels good to get it off my chest. Or maybe it just feels good to get it off my chest to her.

"You don't have a Plan B?"

"I never needed one. I was supposed to be a sure thing."

"What's your major?"

"Business."

"Why business?"

"My parents own a chain of hardware stores. My siblings and I will inherit it someday, so business made sense."

She rises on her elbow. "Then you do have a Plan B."

"I guess. Just not one I've ever really had to consider. I was supposed to be a Major League ballplayer and make millions of dollars to support my family forever." I flop on my back. "Jesus. I sound like a privileged asshole right now, don't I?"

"You sound like someone who's had to live up to a lot of expectations and been lucky enough to never face the uncertainty of failing. It doesn't make you an asshole to be freaked out."

My heart does that jumpy thing again. I force a laugh to cover it up. "My coach wasn't quite as understanding when he yelled at me for moping around today."

"What did he say?"

"To cheer up or get the fuck off his team."

Her quiet puff of laughter is warm against my cheeks, followed by the cool, minty scent of her toothpaste. I can't help myself. I reach up and brush my finger across her bottom lip. "You know what I really want?"

The tiny shake of her head is barely visible in the darkness.

"I want to just not think about it. All I ever do is think and stress about it. I can't get away from it. I want to fucking hide from the entire world—my parents, my coaches, the rankings, the press. Just for a while, you know?"

She nods without speaking, and now I do feel like a loser. I just dragged her from a goddamned pantry, for fuck's sake, where she's been hiding for three months. And all I can do is whine about how hard my life is?

But something shifts in the air between us. She looks at me, lips parted. Her breathing picks up. The stirring low in my gut tells me I need to start picturing nuns if I don't want to embarrass both of us. But then her eyes drop to my mouth, and I'm definitely not picturing nuns.

"Bree."

"What?" she asks, breathy.

"I didn't ask permission before, so I'm doing it now."

Her eyes widen.

"Can I kiss you?"

Her nod is a whisper against the pillowcase, but the desire flaring in her eyes is clear. Beneath the blanket, my hand finds her hip. Just that simple contact sends my heart into a gallop. Then I rise on my elbow to gaze down at her. The sensation of falling strikes again. Like I've been standing on the edge of a cliff and finally decide to jump.

"Jax," she whispers, her face titling up to mine.

I lower my head and nudge her lips. She sighs and opens her mouth to me. I kiss her slowly, deeply, with a laziness that belies the urgent fire raging in my veins. My hand slides up and down her body, over lush curves and valleys. There's so much to dissect between us, but not now. Not tonight.

Tonight, I want to forget everything—my failing career, her heartbreaking realities. I want to isolate myself in the feel of her body, the sounds of her pleasure, the warm embrace of her heat. I want to lose myself in her the way I did that night on the beach.

But I can't. She's vulnerable, and I don't want her vulnerable. I want her passionate and certain.

I pull back and press my forehead to hers. "Go to sleep," I rasp. "We'll figure things out in the morning." Then I roll over, hard and aching.

I feel her tentative touch on my back. "Goodnight," she whispers.

I draw her hand around me so she's spooning my back. Her warm, soft body curls into mine, a perfect fit. I don't know how she does it, but she falls asleep while I remain a tense ball of hormones, shame, and longing.

I might not be much of a baseball prospect anymore, but maybe I can be hers. I just have to convince her to give me a chance.

12

BREE

A QUIET BEEP, beep, beep intrudes on the most amazing dream of my life. I was in Jax's arms, warm and safe, and—my eyes fly open.

What time is it? Where am I?

Confusion sends me up on my elbows until reality seeps back in. It wasn't a dream. I'm here, in his room and his bed. I look over at him, sound asleep next to me with his arm draped across my lap. I recline again and roll closer to him. Every inch of my body still hums and purrs from his kiss last night. Except my chest. I don't know what's going on in there, but things are achy and swollen and kind of shaky. Which is exactly what I feared.

The beep, beep, beep intrudes again, and I realize it's the alarm on his phone. I try to move his arm off my waist so I can get up and deal with it, but he mumbles something and tugs me closer.

"Jax," I giggle.

"Mmmm."

I lean forward and tentatively brush my fingers down his soft beard. He stirs awake and fixes his sleepy gaze on me. His hand slides up my body.

"Jax, your alarm is going off."

He blinks fully awake, makes a grumpy noise, and rolls out of bed to turn it off. I sit up and follow him with my eyes, tracking all the tiny details of his life in the room. A phone charger on the dresser is coiled next to a set of keys and a beaten-up Red Sox hat. A clothes basket by the bathroom door is half-full with laundry, including his wet clothes from last night. In front of it on the floor are a pair of dusty cleats. I imagine him walking through the room, dropping stuff, undressing, going through the manly motions of his day.

He turns around, rubbing a weary hand over his hair. "Sorry. I meant to turn that off last night so it wouldn't wake you up. I usually get up early to run."

"I know. It's OK. I don't want to mess up your routine."

He gives me a small, seductive smile. "Trust me. I've never wanted to stay in bed as much as I want to right now."

My skin overheats. I tear my eyes away from his stuff to where my duffel bag blocks the door. "I, um, I can just get changed real quick and—"

"No. Stay here. I won't be gone long. What, um, what time do you have to be in the kitchen?"

"I'm off today." I shrug. "So, we might as well sneak me and my stuff out now before anyone else gets up."

"Leave your stuff. Otherwise we'll have to drag it all up again."

I wince. "Jax, I can't stay here again."

"Why not?"

"Because this is hardly a permanent solution."

"Well, I'm not letting you sleep in your car!"

I scoot off the bed and walk to him. His hands reach for my hips almost instinctively. I get weak at his touch but find my voice. "Jax, I really appreciate last night. But I have to figure this out on my own."

"Why?"

"I just do." I look away. He doesn't understand.

He slips his finger under my chin and nudges me back to meet his gaze. "Ask Mrs. C today to see if she can get you a room here."

"I can't."

"Why not?"

Because what if she turns me away? I hold the unbidden thought inside. It's bad enough that he discovered my living situation. I don't even want to think about how he'll look at me if he learns the whole, sad truth.

Jax pulls me flush against his body and wraps his arms around me in a warm embrace. "Will you at least promise me one thing?"

"What?"

"If you don't get it figured out, you'll stay with me?"

"OK."

He pulls back and looks down at me. I want him to kiss me like last night, and I don't need to see the desire in his eyes to know he does, too. I feel it in the tightly coiled muscles in his arms. I feel it in the way his hands snake down my back to toy with the hem of my t-shirt just below my butt. I feel it in the hard bulge pressing against my stomach.

I want to rise on tiptoe and mold my mouth to his. I want to slide my hands under his shirt and feel that hot skin.

I want to live in the moment.

Which is why I step back. "Can I use your shower while you're running?"

He lets out a breath and runs his hands through his hair. He looks pained. "Yeah. Sure."

I sit on the bed while he gets ready to head out for his run. He disappears into the bathroom for a few minutes and then emerges in different clothes. He sits down next to me on the mattress to lace up his running shoes. He's a solid mass of man and muscle, and I can't stop watching the way his tight-fitting shirt flexes and tugs over every bulge. My lady parts start to throb and encourage naughty things. *Easy, girl.*

He sits up and looks over at me. "You OK?"

Oh, yeah. Sure. Just, you know, having a little conversation with my vagina. I clear my throat. "Good."

He hesitates, staring openly at my lips. Like he wants to kiss me goodbye.

I don't mean to lean, but I think I do. Because the next thing I know, his lips are on mine. It's just a brief kiss, a soft brush of mouth on mouth, but it's so achingly sweet that I let out a little squeak.

He pulls back with a smile. "What was that?"

"Nothing."

He grins and stands up. "I'll run fast."

I scoot back in bed and watch him leave, a pang of tangled emotions in my chest. It would be so easy to hide from the world with him. To give in to this wild attraction. He wants me as much as I want him.

I thought getting caught in the pantry was the worst thing that could happen to me. I was right, just maybe not for the reasons I originally thought.

Staying with Jax is not an option. He's a clear and present danger to all my careful plans, which means I only have a few hours to figure it out myself.

So I rise, change into my still-damp clothes, pack my bag, and sneak out before he can return.

13

BREE

I ADMIT IT. I'm a wimp. I drive around for three hours, sit by the water, chew on my fingernails, until I can't put it off any longer. I finally return to the house.

I'm too nervous to bother with small talk as I march into the kitchen to find Mrs. C. "Can I talk to you?"

Mrs. C looks up from the stock pot on the stove where she's dumping chopped veggies into broth.

The corners of her lips twitch. "Well, it's about damn time, girl."

I blink. "What?"

Mrs. C adjusts the burner under the pot and wipes her hands on a towel. "Stay here."

She walks to her small office adjacent to the kitchen and returns a few minutes later, a puffy envelope in her hand. I know without asking what's in it. When you spend your entire life desperate for money, you know what it looks like.

"You're not making up an excuse this year," she says, handing it to me.

"Wh-what?"

"The contest. There's enough in there for you to enter two recipes." She raises her eyebrows. "That *is* what you wanted to talk to me about, right?"

If I weren't so shocked, I'd laugh. Except now I've officially lost my nerve now for the other thing. Humiliation and shame make me lie with a nod. I take the envelope with a trembling hand. "I'll pay you back."

"I wouldn't want you to, but it's not just me. There are donations from twenty people in there, and I'm not giving you any of their names."

"People donated?" I cringe. I hate feeling like a charity case.

"People who care about you, yes."

Mrs. C smooths her apron. "Now, since you're here, I've got a basket full of brownies and other treats for the boys. Why don't you take it over to the practice field for me since you're going to be heading downtown to enter the contest anyway."

I remain rooted in place as she walks to the prep counter and grabs the basket for me.

She walks back with one of her looks. "You know, sometimes we simply have to take the risk of trusting people." She holds out the basket.

I nod and walk out before she sees me cry.

14

JAX

I CROUCH DOWN, waiting for the pitcher to throw. I'm still in the bullpen, but I don't care as much right now.

Because she left.

I can't fucking believe it. I ran hard and fast only to return to an empty room. When I ran back down to the parking lot, I realized her car was gone, too. Then when I grabbed my phone to text her, I remembered I don't even have her fucking phone number. Where the hell did she go?

I stand and lift my face mask and swipe my arm across my brow. It's hot as balls. Whatever cold front had been hanging over the area was pushed out by last night's storm. I look down at my arm—sweaty and brown with grime from my face. I'm going to need about five showers before Bree comes back to my room tonight.

If she comes back.

Grady saunters over and points to something behind me. "Dude, your girl is here."

"What?" I whip around and feel my heart leap into my throat as relief floods my limbs. Bree stands by the dugout, surrounded by ten of my teammates. She's holding out a basket full of something that the guys are practically fighting over.

Grady snorts and punches my arm. "Shit, man. You should see your face right now."

I cough to cover my reaction. "Why?"

"You look like you're ten years old and just met Derek Jeter."

"Fuck off," I snort. But it's probably an accurate description.

Grady nods back in Bree's direction. "Look at them. She's like their team mom or something."

Something protective and embarrassingly possessive rises inside me. I want to claim her like a cave man. I turn away from Grady and head toward Bree. She looks up from the basket and... ah, God. That shy little smile. My heart erupts.

One of the first-years sees me coming, stands up straight, and takes off. The rest follow, all shooting me sorry-don't-kill-me looks as they run.

"Hi," I say, stopping just close enough to be *close enough* without embarrassing her.

"Hi." She worries her lip with her teeth.

"You left."

"I know."

"I was worried. I don't even have your phone number."

Her cheeks burn pink. "Sorry." She holds out the basket. "Mrs. C sent me over with some goodies."

"Goodies, huh?"

She turns a darker shade of pink. God, she's killing me. "So, does that mean you talked to her?"

Her eyes crinkle at the corners for a second before she shakes her head. "I tried." A story tumbles from her mouth about Mrs. C assuming she was asking for help with some recipe contest.

"So, you still don't have a place to stay?"

She shakes her head again, looking everywhere but at me.

"Then stay with me."

"Jax, I can't do that."

"Why not?"

"Because we, because you—" She lets out a frustrated breath.

I take a step closer and lower my voice. "Because we're attracted to each other and might act on it?"

"Yes."

"Would that be so bad?" I hold up my hands. "Wait. Don't answer that. My ego is kind of fragile these days."

She laughs quietly. I take it as a good sign. "What if we go out tonight?"

She arches an eyebrow."Like a—like a date?"

"Exactly like a date."

"Why?"

"Besides the obvious reasons?"

"Yeah."

An idea takes root that might convince her. "Because you'll be doing me a favor. I'm trying not to think about my life, remember? I need the distraction."

Her eyes glance right while she thinks.

"I have an idea." I take another step closer. "When was the last time you had a picnic on the beach while watching Avengers movies on a laptop?"

She bursts out another laugh. "Um, definitely never."

"That ends today."

Her smile fills up my chest with a buoyancy I've never experi-
enced before.

Coach's voice ruins the moment. "Tanner! Stop flirting and get
back to work!"

The blush reappears on her cheeks. "I got you in trouble.
Sorry."

"Nah. He yells at everyone like that. I probably should get back
to it, though."

"K," she murmurs, clutching the basket.

I step closer, wrap my fingers around her elbow, and tug her
closer. She fits so perfectly against me. "Meet me in our special
spot at eight."

Her mouth drops open, and I mentally kick myself. Was that
too much? But then she smiles again and nods. I watch her walk
through the gate next to the dugout. Then I turn and jog back to the
bullpen.

"Tanner!"

I stop and look toward home plate. Coach is giving me that
arms-crossed glare again. I change directions and jog to him
instead. "Yeah, Coach?"

"You want to flirt, do it on your own time."

"Yes, sir. Sorry."

Coach spits out a shell. "Just heard back from your docs.
You're good to go, but they sent over some stretches they want you
to do."

I nod, my eyes drifting back toward the gate where Bree left. I
have to make tonight special.

"You listening to me, son?"

I drag my eyes back to Coach. "Yes, sir."

"I got two more calls this morning."

"OK."

He cocks an eyebrow. "That's it? You're not going to grill me about which teams or which round?"

"Nope."

"What's going on with you, kid?"

"Nothing, sir. I just don't give a shit."

Because the only thing I care about is getting Bree back to our beach and doing it right this time with her.

I might be a fool for trying to hide from the real world, for pretending nothing else matters. But if I can get Bree back in my arms, it might be worth it.

The right girl always is.

15

BREE

I CAN'T BELIEVE we're back here, sitting on a blanket in our private circle of trees.

I can't believe he called it *our spot*.

I can't believe I said *yes*.

"OK, I have a chicken salad wrap or a ham and cheese wrap. Which one do you want?" I brought a picnic basket full of more food than we could possibly eat because I was nervous all afternoon, and this is what I do when I'm nervous—make food. If Mrs. C was suspicious about what I was doing in her kitchen, she didn't mention it. Thank God.

Jax stretches his legs out next to his laptop, which is paused on the opening credits of some superhero movie. "Which one do *you* want?"

"Nope. You choose."

He leans forward to grab the ham and cheese, but instead of

settling back with his sandwich, he kisses me. "Thank you for making all this."

"I didn't want you to be hungry."

"I'm always going to be hungry around you."

I'm starting to understand what it means to swoon, because I suddenly feel faint. I give him a small, playful shove, and he falls back to the blanket with a laugh.

I hand him a bag of chips, a plastic container of pasta salad, and a bottle of red pop. He looks at the bottle skeptically. "This is a Michigan thing, isn't it?"

"Try it. You've never tasted anything so good."

He arches an eyebrow over dark eyes. "That sounds like a challenge."

Oh, boy.

I watch Jax dig into his food. After a moment, he looks up. "What? Do I have food on my face?"

"I like to watch you eat."

He laughs. "Why?"

"Because—" I shut up, embarrassed.

Jax sets his food down and crawls over to me. "Why?" he asks, mouth close to mine.

"Because it makes me happy when you like something I made."

He blinks, a tender expression replacing the flirtatious one from before. "That's actually kind of sweet."

I look away. I can deal with flirtatious, but tender kills me. It was the *tender* that pushed me over the cliff of bad decisions the last time we were alone in this spot.

I pick at my food while he finishes his. Then I gather up our trash and dirty dishes and return them to the picnic basket.

Jax leans back against the trunk of a tree and holds out his arm. "Come here."

I crawl over to him, heart pounding, and settle against his side.

"I've never seen any Marvel movies," I admit, mostly to distract myself from the intoxicating heat of being so close to him.

Jax laughs. "I can basically recite every Iron Man movie ever made."

"Is Iron Man in this one?"

He laughs again. "Yeah. He's an Avenger."

"Superman?"

"He's a DC superhero."

"I have no idea what you're talking about."

Jax slides his arm down to my waist and tugs me closer. "Someday, we'll have a movie marathon, and I'll show you all the Avengers movies."

Someday. How can a single word be packed with so much poignant hope? No one has ever wanted a *someday* with me.

Jax tells me the name of each superhero as they appear. He keeps his arm around me, and I eventually lay my head on his shoulder. I feel like I'm being protected by my own personal Captain America. I want to close my eyes and enjoy the feel of him wrapped around me inside this dark nest. Is this how other people feel all the time? Safe and wanted?

I snuggle deeper against his chest. "You're so warm. I could fall asleep like this."

"Sleep, if you want."

"That would make me the worst date ever."

He bends to nuzzle my ear. "Holding you while you sleep would be the best date ever. I know, because I did it last night."

My insides melt into warm honey. I could get used to this, which would be dangerous. Shoulder injury or not, he's still a prospect. He's still eligible. He's still going to leave. And he said it himself. I'm just a distraction from his current problems.

Yet here I am, curled up in his embrace in our special spot, dreaming of somedays and movie marathons in his arms. I can't afford to fall farther for him than I already have. I fell two years ago and never got up. I've been limping, hiding the injury ever since. I won't survive another wound, but it feels too good right now to worry how much it might hurt later.

Maybe that's what Lexi means by living in the moment.

Maybe that's what Jax means by hiding from the world for a while.

Or maybe I'm just looking for an excuse for dangling on that cliff again, because I'm on the precipice of another reckless decision.

"What are you thinking about?" he murmurs against my hair.

"The last time we were here."

Jax nuzzles my hair. "So am I."

"What are you thinking?" My voice is airy, breathless.

"That I wish I'd done things differently." His is deep, serious.

"Differently how?"

"I wish I'd taken things slower. I moved too fast, and it scared you off."

I ease away from his body and look up. My tenuous grip on solid ground slips even more at the intensity in his gaze. "We both moved fast that night. I'm as much to blame as you are. Running away and refusing to talk to you was childish. I'm sorry."

A gentle smile softens the lines of his lips. "I'm sorry, too."

"For what?"

"For making you think you *couldn't* talk to me."

I lift my shoulder in a half-hearted shrug. "I don't really talk to anyone. We all hide in our own ways, I guess."

His fingers splay wider against my waist. "What do you hide from?"

Abandonment. The word hovers on my tongue, sour and shameful, like a dirty little secret. I run and hide from the fear of ever feeling again the way I did so many times as a child, the way I did the night Brett tossed me a suitcase and made it clear I was worth nothing more than the few tattered items I could fit in it.

But what I fear more than the feeling itself is admitting it to anyone. So, I do what I always do in response to Jax's question.

I lie.

"Same things you do," I say, aiming for a convincing tone. "From the future. From my own thoughts. All I do is think and worry. Every second of every day. It's exhausting." At least that part is true.

Jax's face dips closer to mine. "Then maybe we can hide together for a while."

For a while. Those three words should be enough to bring me back to my senses, but they don't. Instead, I'm stuck on a different word. *Together.* What a gift of a word for a girl like me. My fingers curl into his t-shirt. "That sounds perfect."

"Good." He lowers his forehead to mine. "Because the next move is up to you, Bree."

This is my chance to save myself from falling, but I don't want to.

Because I want to hide. I want the mirage. I want *together.*

Even if it's only for a while.

16

JAX

SOMEHOW, despite the pounding of my heart, I remain still as Bree brushes her mouth across mine. Her lips are warm, her touch shy. She explores me with whispered kisses and fluttering fingers.

It's lazy. It's hot. It's going to fucking kill me if I don't touch her soon.

But I hold back, keep my hand locked firmly at her waist, because I won't make the same mistake I made before. I won't let my raging desire push us both too quickly into something that sends her running away again. I have to let her set the pace this time.

Bree finally pulls away with a shy smile that makes my heart grow twice its size. And when she lifts her t-shirt over her head and lowers herself to the blanket, it begins to pound with enough force to make me breathless. I rise on his knees, hot and tight, to whip off my own shirt. She squeaks, her eyes drifting up and down my torso.

"Wow," she breathes.

Pure male ego sends my desire into overdrive. "You just made every fucking minute I spend in the gym worth it."

Bree laughs as I lower my body to cover hers. Her laugh fades into a quiet moan as the coarse hair of my chest abrades the soft skin of hers.

I press my mouth to her ear. "I want to do it right this time."

"You did it right the first time."

Her skin beckons, and I dip my tongue into the tiny crest behind her ear. "No, I didn't. I was such a fucking fool that night. I should have held you and kissed every inch of you."

I trace my tongue along her collarbone. She shivers and whispers my name.

"I didn't take my time." I kiss her throat. "I didn't taste you." I slide my hand up her flat abdomen until I brush the swell of her breast with my fingertips. "I didn't savor you."

I shove aside the cup of her bra and capture a taut, pink nipple in my mouth. She moans and slides her leg over my hip. I suck and lick until her fingers dig into my back.

I move down her body, kissing a trail as I go until my legs hang over the blanket onto the sand. Until I meet the wet mound hidden by her simple, white panties.

Bree lets out a small, surprised cry.

I look up at her and nearly explode in my own shorts. Her face is tilted toward the sky, eyes closed, an expression of rapture decorating her features.

She turns her gaze down to mine, and the gentle trust in her eyes steals the breath from my lungs.

"I should have made sure you knew that everything you were feeling, I was feeling, too."

A small breath escapes on a gentle "oh" from her lips.

"But what I really did wrong," I whisper, licking the exposed skin above the waistband of her panties, "is that I didn't get to know your body."

I slide my hands up her thighs and stop to tease my thumbs over her mound. "You didn't come, did you?"

"I-I didn't know how," she pants, hands digging into the blanket beneath us.

I tease her with the tip of my finger, tucking it just under the panty line to caress her curls. "Do you know how now?"

She shakes her head, a pink tinge rising on her cheeks. "You're the only man I've ever been with."

I press my lips again to her mound. She whimpers and shifts her hips, pressing into my mouth. My hands grip her underwear and inch them down slowly, kissing as I go until my lips reach her tangle of dark curls.

She whimpers again. I look up. "Do you want me to stop?"

"No," she breathes.

I part her with my fingers and slide the pad of my thump up and down the soft length of her. The next moan I hear is mine, because my cock swells into a painful throb. I find her clit and circle it. She starts to cry out but slaps a hand over her mouth.

"Right there," I groan. "Let me kiss me you there."

"Yes," she moans.

I hold her open with my fingers so I can press my lips against her. Her legs shake, her hips buck. I flick my tongue over her, back and forth, up and down. Then I pause to suck, kiss, suck again.

"Jax, oh God..." Her legs tremble. Her hand grips the back of my head.

I pull back to look at her face. My thumb circles her again and again. She throws her head back, pants. Squeezes my shoulder. She whimpers my name. Her toes curl into the blanket.

"Tell me. Tell me how to take you over."

She groans. "I don't know."

I grab her legs, loop them over my shoulders, and bury my face between them. I suck, kiss, lick until she's writhing beneath me. I slide two fingers inside her and pump in time with my tongue, and fuck, FUCK. I can feel her muscles start to contract from the inside. Holy shit, I didn't even know that was possible.

Her legs suddenly stiffen. Her hips lift against my mouth.

And with a wrenching, muffled cry, she arches her back off the blanket and gives herself over to it.

She trembles and whimpers. "Jax, that was … " She doesn't finish the sentence. Her head falls back, legs still trembling.

I rise to my knees, frantic. I have to get inside her. I shed my shorts and my boxer briefs, pausing to grab the condom from my pocket before throwing my shorts to the side. She slips out of her bra and flings it.

She watches as I sheath myself, and then she reaches for me with a smile. I thought the ache in my cock was bad, but that smile … my chest explodes. I claim her mouth and devour her with my kiss, the taste of her still on my tongue. I can't wait any longer. I need to feel her wrapped around me.

"Bree…" I groan into her neck. "I have to be inside you."

Her legs fall open, and I find her opening with a single thrust. The shock of it, of how fucking good she feels after all this time, brings a growl from low in my throat. I'm lost in her.

Bracing myself on my hands, I rise so I can stare down at her. "So beautiful," I moan, and she gives me that smile again. A joy I don't recognize bubbles just beneath the throbbing ache.

I bury my face in her shoulder and lose myself. Pumping in and out until I'm mindless for her, until the pulse and pull of her intimate muscles as she reaches her second orgasm send me over the edge. A noise I've never made before bursts from my throat as I explode in wave after wave of the most mind-blowing pleasure I've ever felt.

I collapse on top of her and try to breathe. Try to think.

Try not to panic.

An emotion I can't identify seizes my lungs. "Bree ... I'm afraid to let you go this time."

Her arms come around me in an almost comforting embrace. "Then take me home."

Home.

I close my eyes, that emotion choking me now. I cough to shake it off. "Home sounds great."

17

JAX

IT TAKES some serious cloak-and-dagger shit, but we figure out a plan to get her back to my room without being caught. She goes in through the service door while I run around to the front. I wait at the top of the back stairs for her.

When she reaches me, I grab her hand, drag her into my room, wrap an arm her waist, and kick the door shut behind us. I toss her bag on the floor and then tug her shirt over her head.

The rest of our clothes follow quickly, and I back her toward the bed. She sits down, scoots back, and reaches for me. I cover myself in a condom and enter her in a single, clumsy thrust.

Her back arches off the bed as her legs come around my waist. I feel frantic. Desperate. Her nails dig into my back. My hands clench the sheets. I don't know what's happening, but something has taken hold of me. Something animalistic. Primal. I can't go hard enough, deep enough, or fast enough to satisfy my hunger for her.

Her orgasm hits so hard and fast that I nearly collapse at the intense pleasure of it. Her muscles pulse and contract around me, sending me flying over that cliff with her. My elbows give out.

I start to pull out, but she winds her arms around my neck. "Stay," she whispers. "Just for a second."

For a second? I'll stay forever, if she'll let me. In all my life, I've never known a moment more perfect than this. I'm heavy on top of her, my face burrowed deep into the pocket of her neck. But she doesn't seem to mind.

"Mmm," she says, warm and pliant.

"Tired?"

"Mmm."

I turn my lips to her hair. "Sleep, if you want."

"Worst date ever."

"Best date ever."

She sinks into the bed. I hold her until her breathing slows. Just like last night. She falls asleep faster than anyone I've ever known. Maybe it's because it has been so long since she's had a decent place to sleep. And on that thought, my throat thickens. I can't believe she's been living in a damn closet for three months. *I don't really talk to anyone.* The loneliness of that admission combined with the image of her pantry secret is a death sentence to my emotions.

With a quite cough, I finally ease out of her body. I dispose of the condom in the bathroom and return to Bree. She curls against my side, hand on my chest.

I let her sleep for a few minutes before rolling us both into a better position. But as soon as I do, my phone trills somewhere in the pocket of my pants on the floor. It's my mom's text tone. I ignore it, because *shudder*. The thought of reading a text from my mom right now is enough to cause permanent limp dick.

Bree stirs, and her hand slides down my chest. "It's OK if you want to check that."

I capture her hand with mine. "I don't."

The phone dings again. "Maybe you should check it."

"It's my mom. If I pick up the phone right now, I'll probably accidentally hit FaceTime and scar us both for life."

Bree's tired laughter fills up the room until I feel like I'm floating. I pull her hand to my mouth and press a kiss to the palm. "You should laugh more."

"You make me laugh."

"Yeah?" I slide my hand down to squeeze the perfect curve her ass. "I like making you make all kinds of noises."

Her laugh this time is low and seductive and sparks a tug low in my gut. It hasn't even been fifteen minutes, but my body is already stirring for another go. I didn't even know that was possible.

Her lips creep along my pec, and when her tongue darts out and circles my nipple, my hips buck instinctively. Holy fuck. If I'd known how fucking good that felt, I would've spent a helluva lot more time doing it to her.

Bree shifts quickly until she's on top of me, and suddenly, our hands move everywhere at once, mouths devouring each other. Her legs widen over my hips as she rises to straddle me. An oath escapes on an exhale as I stare up at her.

"Is this OK?" she asks quietly.

"Fuck, yes. Why would you even ask?"

"You have a look on your face."

"It's because you're so fucking beautiful."

Her smile spreads wide across her face. "Oh…"

My hands slide up her body and cover her breasts. Her eyes drift closed as I flick each nipple with my thumbs. She starts to move, hips undulating against my erection. With one thrust I could be inside her. Before I lose my fucking mind and do just that, I reach over to fumble for a condom from the table next to the bed—and damn near fall off as my phone rings.

Bree opens her eyes and looks down at me, lips curled up at the corners. "Your mom?"

I groan and drop my head to the pillow. "Don't even say that word right now."

She laughs again—God, I love the way it sounds. She leans forward, drops a quick kiss on my lips, and slides off me. "Answer it," she whispers. "It might be important."

"She just wants to make sure I haven't died from carbon monoxide poisoning."

Bree laughs again. I grunt as I sit, my erection bobbing like a fucking buoy in the middle of Lake Michigan. My phone lights up the fabric of the pocket.

I pull it out. "Hey."

"Geez, there you are. I was starting to worry you had died from carbon monoxide poisoning."

I smile even though I'm sitting here naked with a raging hard-on and a very naked Bree behind me. "You probably would've gotten a call from someone if that happened," I deadpan.

"I just wanted to hear how things are going. You're settled in?"

"Yeah. Everything's good."

"How's your shoulder? Are you icing it and stretching?"

"Yep." I twist and look over my shoulder. Bree smiles. "Can I call you back tomorrow? I'm, uh, about to go to bed."

Bree bites her lip, and fuuuuck. I reach for her breast. She shakes her heads, eyes round, and slides away. I wink and turn back around as my mom responds.

"That's fine. Or just text me. You know I start imagining the worst if I don't hear from you."

"I know. But I promise I'm watching for deer when I drive, and I won't go swimming after I've been drinking, and I'm pretty sure this place has decent smoke detectors."

She tsks. "What about carbon monoxide detectors?"

"Those, too."

"OK, honey. Get some sleep. We love you."

"Love you, too."

I end the call, drop the phone onto my pants on the floor, and turn around. I find Bree smiling at me, not seductively like before, but all sweet-like.

"What?" I say, reclining and reaching for her at the same time.

She scoots to my side and props herself on her elbow. "That was cute."

"So are you." I slide my hand up her back to circle her neck and try to pull her down. "Where were we?"

She tugs back. "Nuh-uh. I want to hear about your family."

"*Now*?!"

She laughs. "Yes, now."

It's the laugh that gets me. "Fine," I grumble, but I wink at her so she knows I'm kidding. I tuck an arm beneath my head. "What do you want to know?"

She shrugs. "I don't have a lot of experience with big families, so…"

"They're great," I say, gently squeezing the back of her neck. "They can be annoying sometimes like any family, I guess, but I definitely hit a home run in that department."

She smiles. "Who's your favorite sibling?"

"I hate them all."

She laughs again. "Liar."

"Yeah, I'm lying. I'm closest to my brother, Gabe, I guess, because he's only a year younger than me. But my little sisters," I pause, smiling. I've never really thought about this before. "I'm really protective of them. Allison is three years younger and Hannah is five years younger."

"Protective how?"

I give a one-shouldered shrug. "I don't know. Just, you know, checking out the guys they date and stuff. Hannah went to prom for the first time this year. I went home for the weekend so I could see her in her dress and shit, and she was so mad because I kept glaring at her date."

Bree blinks. "You went home from college just to see your sister in her prom dress?"

"Yeah. Why?"

"Isn't it a long drive from Ohio State to your hometown?"

"Yeah, but she's my youngest sibling, and my parents make a big deal out of that kind of stuff. My mom insists on getting family photos and all that. And anyway, it worked out. We had an away game that weekend at Penn State, which is just a half hour from home."

She smiles softly. "You really love them, don't you?"

My chest constricts again. "I do."

She smiles again and then lays down to rest in the circle of my arm. I tighten my hold on her, knocked mute for a moment at how perfect it feels. Her hand finds a place on my stomach, and her fingers toy with the hair around my belly button.

"Do you tell them that a lot?"

"Tell them what?"

"That you love them?"

My heart pinches again. Why would she ask that? "Yeah, I do."
I pause. "Don't you tell your family that?"

Her fingers grow still against my stomach. "My mom died
when I was little, and I don't have any siblings, so … "

"What about your stepdad?"

"Of course. We say it all the time on the phone."

"Do you talk to him a lot?"

"Sure."

"Then why isn't he helping you?"

I barely get the sentence out, because her hand slides down my
body. "Let's not talk anymore," she says.

I roll her over and capture her mouth with mine. But even as
she drives all coherent thought from my mind, one remains.

Maybe she's hiding from more than the future. Maybe it's the
past she wants to avoid.

18

BREE

THE ALARM WAKES me up again, and this time I know exactly where I am.

I roll into Jax and kiss him. He awakens with a low, satisfied sound, weaving his fingers into my hair to hold me tighter.

I laugh against his mouth. "Your alarm is going off again."

"You have no idea," he says in a sleepy, sexy voice as he rolls me over and wedges his thigh between my legs. The thick weight of his erection rests against my hip bone, probing and promising.

The alarm goes off louder this time.

He groans. "Hang on."

I openly gape as he stands up and crosses the room to the dresser where he set his phone last night to charge before we fell asleep. I swallow to keep from drooling. I didn't see him like this before—on full display. He's perfect. Sculpted and masculine. Smooth and rough.

I feel bad for lying to him last night about Brett, but I wasn't ready for his inevitable pity. He's my oasis. Why ruin it with reality?

Jax turns back around, and my eyes drop from the dark hair covering his bulging pecs to the single line of hair that leads to his erection jutting out from his body. His smile turns naughty. "I could get used to you looking at me like that."

Heat races up my cheeks. He crawls back into bed and draws back the covers to expose my body. His eyes take their time traveling the full length of me. "I don't even know where to start," he murmurs in that same sexy tone. "You're like a breakfast buffet of all my favorites."

I burst out a laugh, but it quickly dies as his mouth lowers to my breast. "When was the last time you had an orgasm," he teases, gently tugging my nipple with his teeth.

"Way too long ago," I moan.

"That ends right now."

It doesn't take long until we're panting and groping and grinding. He fumbles for a condom, and then he eases inside me slowly, inch by inch.

"Are you sore," he whispers against my lips.

"No. Why?"

He gazes down at me with tender concern. "We went at it pretty hard last night. You said you haven't been with anyone in a long time, so ..."

"I haven't been with anyone but *you*," I correct quietly. "And I feel good."

His lips spread into a smile as we kiss. "Yes, you do."

He rolls us both until I'm on top. His hands cover my breasts as I move. I bite my own arm to keep from crying out and waking the whole floor.

"Bree," he moans. "God, baby. You feel so fucking good."

He suddenly sits and wraps his arms around me. The position brings the achiest part of me in direct contact with the hardest part of him. I'm not in control of my own body. My hips rock and grind, lift and lower. Sweat drips down my back. His hands dig into my ass and lift me higher, faster, harder.

"Jax!" His name escapes my lips on a cry that I can't muffle. "Oh God. Oh God."

I stiffen as waves of pleasure explode along every nerve ending. He groans and thrusts deeper into me, and then together we collapse, falling to our sides, legs still entwined.

He slips from my body but draws me against his chest, hand cupping my head. "Bree ... Baby, that was ..." He laughs. "I don't even know what that was."

I do. It was mind-blowing, life-changing, totally inconvenient, fall-in-love-with-you sex.

"I won't need to go running in the morning anymore if we keep this up," he pants.

He's teasing, but I can't find it in myself to laugh. How long are we going to *keep this up*? How long before my attempts to keep my heart out of it prove futile? How long can I hide from reality, from my own feelings? How long until the novelty wears off for him and I become a burden again?

I pull the blanket over us and hold him. There's an emotion radiating off him I can't identify, but I feel it, too. It seeps from his body into mine, soaking into every cell. Under the blanket, he finds my hand again and wraps it within his. It's too sweet. Too affectionate. Too addictive.

"Bree."

"Mmmm?"

"What's wrong?"

"Nothing," I lie.

He rises on his elbows, bracketing my face in his hands as he looks down. "Talk to me."

I run my hands up his spine. "Just thinking about where I'll stay tonight."

He draws his eyebrows together. "Here."

"I can't stay here forever, Jax."

He blinks a couple of times, expression blank. "But you can stay tonight."

My heart splinters at his answer, and then I hate myself when I realize why. Part of me had been hoping, *naively* hoping, that he'd beg for forever. I force a smile. "OK. I can stay tonight."

"And tomorrow," he says, dropping a kiss on my mouth. "I'll convince you stay then, too."

"Oh, yeah? You sure about that?"

"One day at a time, babe," he says, kissing me again. "That's all we have to worry about."

One day at a time.

If he can do it, so can I.

And now I'm even lying to myself.

19

JAX

"You ignored me last night."

I'm on my back on the field, stretching my leg across my body. I block the sun with my hand to look up at Grady. Our fourth home game of the season is today, and his white uniform glares like a reflection off the water.

"What are you talking about?"

Grady drops down next to me to go through the same stretching routine. "I texted you about going out, and you ignored me."

"I was busy."

He snorts. "Yeah, no shit. Whatever happened to *she's off-fucking-limits?*"

"I changed my mind." I smile just thinking about her. I'm like a high school kid with his first girlfriend. It's been ten one-day-at-a-times so far. Somehow, I keep convincing her to stay. We've even perfected a routine of hiding her car and sneaking her upstairs. Only Grady knows that she's staying in my room.

"You gotta come up for air soon, man. Hang with your boys."

I roll over to stretch my quads. "Sorry. You feeling neglected?"

"Yeah, man. I'm starting to question our relationship and your feelings for me."

"I'll send you flowers."

He snorts again. "Well, whatever you're doing—or, I guess, *she's* doing—"

I shoot him a glare.

"Keep doing it," he finishes. "Because you're officially in beast mode."

I stand and start my arm swings. He's right. I haven't played this well since before the injury. I guess the answer to my problems was to stop thinking about them.

Bullshit. The answer to my problems was Bree.

Which is its own problem, because she's really into the one-day-at-a-time thing. I'm ready to talk about all kinds of tomorrows, but she avoids all my attempts to discuss it. *We're supposed to be hiding from the future, right?* That's what she said just this morning. I enjoy the avoidance, too, but the calendar doesn't care. The draft will be here before we know it.

"Tanner!"

I look over my shoulder at Coach. "Why does he always yell my name like that?"

"I don't know," Grady snorts. "But I'm glad he's after you and not me."

I jog toward the dugout. "What's up, Coach?"

"I'm starting Frasier on the mound today. He's freaking out, so you gotta coach him up. He's puking in the bathroom right now."

I grimace. "Can I at least wait until he's done?"

Coach smirks. "He's a smart kid. He could learn a lot from you. So, keep your head in the game and help him through it today. Yeah?"

I nod and start to head back toward the field.

"Hey."

I turn around. Coach clears his throat and crosses his arms. "*Is* your head in the game?"

"What do you mean, sir?"

"I know you're playing well, but I'm not blind. What's going on with you and the McTavish girl?"

Shit. I swallow and consider my answer.

Coach holds up a hand. "Just be careful. You hear me? A girl like her—"

I react without thinking. "Excuse me, sir? What the fuck does *a girl like her* mean?"

"Back it up, kid. I'm giving her a compliment."

I clench my jaw but take a step back.

"What I mean is, she's the kind you don't mess around with. The kind who deserves good things. You hear me?" He spits out a sunflower seed. "Especially her. It's a fucking shame what that bastard did to her."

I blink, not sure if I should admit I have no idea what he's talking about.

"Throws her out on the day of her graduation and says he's done his job, she's on her own from now on?"

Wait. What? Cold dread seeps into my bones. Her stepfather threw her out? On the day of her graduation? "He just abandoned her?"

"Yep." Coach shakes his head. "What kind of father does something like that?"

"Stepfather, you mean."

Coach looks at me like I'm nuts. "Is that what she told you?"

My stomach revolts. "He's her *real* dad?"

Coach spits. "Yep. It's fucked up. Which is why I'm telling you to be careful with her unless you're serious."

All the things that still didn't make sense suddenly do. Her own father threw her out? No wonder she doesn't trust anyone. No wonder she wants to hide from her past.

But then another thought comes to me, and my breakfast makes a full-fledged run for my throat. The day of her graduation. That was the night we made love on the beach. She was vulnerable, and I came along offering something she desperately wanted and needed—someone to love her, even if just for a night. And then I offered to drive her home.

Home.

I think I'm going to be sick.

The urge to run back to her at the house is so strong that I actually take a step.

"You listening to me, Tanner?"

I look back at Coach. He jams a fat finger into the center of my chest guard. "Don't you mess around with Bree McTavish unless you fucking mean it."

A wave of certainty chases away the nausea. I do mean it.

I just have to convince Bree of that.

20

BREE

"You know, at some point you're actually going to have to open your eyes and watch him play."

Lexi nudges me in the stands, but I keep my eyes closed. Jax is at the plate, waiting for a pitch. The game is almost over, and it's tied. If Jax gets a hit, he'll knock in the winning run for the Sluggers.

I've been to every home game so far, but since I closed my eyes the first time I saw him bat, and he hit a home run, I'm now afraid to watch. What if I open my eyes, and he strikes out?

Lexi snorts. "You're as superstitious as they are. You're the perfect baseball girlfriend."

My insides get gooey. "I'm not his girlfriend."

Lexi snorts again. "Right. You just come to every game, and spend every night with him."

I wince. I still haven't told her the whole truth. She's going to be so pissed if she finds out the real reason I'm staying with him. I try to keep my voice light. "You're the one who told me to give him a chance."

"I told you to use him for sex, not fall in love," she laughs.

"I am *not* in love with him." I wait for my pants to burst into flames. I fell in love around day two or three. Lying just helps me hide from the inevitable.

Lexi nudges me again. "Here it comes."

I crack open one eye. The pitcher throws the ball. Jax swings and misses.

"Strike one," the announcer calls.

I squeak and cover my face with my hands.

The next pitch is a ball. I peek out again to see Jax step back from the plate, kick the bat against his cleats, and then take his stance again.

I close my eyes.

And hear a loud crack of the bat.

I peel my hands away in time to watch the ball fly high over the field and out of the park. Jax pumps his arm high and starts running the bases. The crowd is on its feet, cheering and clapping. I watch as the dugout empties and his teammates wait for him at home plate with high fives and bear hugs.

Amid the chaos, he finds me with his eyes and winks.

Lexi and I descend the steps of the bleachers and walk to the chain-link fence that separates players from fans. Jax runs over, sweaty and grimy. His uniform hugs his massive shoulders and powerful legs, and I feel faint just looking at him.

I rest my hands on the grooves at the top of the fence. He bends and drops a kiss to my lips. "Hey."

Lexi fakes a gag. "Someone could go into sugar shock around you two."

I ignore her. "Ice cream?" It's our post-game tradition.

"Of course." He kisses me again. "Give me fifteen minutes."

He races off toward the clubhouse to get cleaned up.

Lexi and I walk toward the front gate of the ballpark, where I always wait for Jax after games. Families and tourists pass us by, buzzing with excitement about the game and the players. It's always like this leading up to draft weekend. Everyone wants to say they were there to watch a future superstar before he's plucked from our tiny field and thrust into Major League destiny. The fact that it could be Jax makes my stomach clench. I don't want him to get drafted. For his sake, of course. He deserves a better shot than a mid-round pick.

I shake my head to clear my thoughts. I don't want to think about the draft.

Lexi and I hop up to sit on the low wall outside the gate and kick our feet against the brick. "So, have you decided which recipes to enter?" she asks.

"I think so. I'm thinking my cherry barbeque sauce and then a Lake Michigan white fish with sautéed morels and cherry compote."

Lexi squees. "You are *so* going to win."

"I doubt it. But it feels good to enter."

"Did you hear who one of the judges is?"

I shake my head. "Who?"

"Dirk Vacho!"

A jolt of adrenaline shoots through me. Dirk Vacho is the head of culinary services for the Beckinsale hotel chain and once served as a judge on a national cooking show. Getting noticed by him could make a chef's career take off overnight. Last year, he judged a recipe contest in California and, on the spot, offered the winner a spot in the Beckinsale Institute—one of the top culinary programs in the world.

Not that it would happen to me, but still. Knowing that he's going to be one of the judges has my head spinning and heart racing.

"So," Lexi says again, and this time there's a lot of heavy meaning behind the word.

"What?"

"Have you guys talked about what you'll do after?"

I play dumb. "What who will do after what?"

"Duh. You and Jax. After the draft. Or after the summer ends. Just, you know, *after*."

"Not really." Not at all. We live in a cocoon of agreed denial.

"But the draft is, like, next weekend." She says it like she's trying to explain it to a first grader.

"I know."

"You haven't talked about what you'll do if he gets sent to a minor league team?"

"No."

"So, if he gets drafted and sent away, you'll what? Just see what happens?"

I shrug, but her questions are starting to wiggle their way inside my protective shell.

"Bree—"

"What?" I snap. "You're always the one telling me to be happy, to just enjoy life for a change. That's what I'm trying to do!"

Lexi jumps like I've slapped her, and guilt washes over me. "I'm sorry. I didn't mean to yell at you."

"No, you're right." Lexi yanks me into a quick hug. "I shouldn't be badgering you. It's just not like you to not totally micromanage every aspect of your life. This seems like a pretty big thing to just leave to fate."

Leave it to Lexi to pick at my biggest scab. "We're not leaving anything to fate. When he leaves, he leaves. That's it."

Lexi blinks at me. "That's it? I don't understand."

"It's a summer fling, Lexi. That's it." The words are sour on my tongue. It's a summer fling for *him*.

Lexi blinks at me like she's considering saying something more. But then she straightens. "Here he comes."

I turn and follow her gaze. Jax lifts his hand in a wave. I get that light-headed, floaty stomach feeling I always get when I see him. He has traded his dirt-covered uniform for army-green shorts and a faded Ohio State t-shirt, and his hair is still wet from his shower. His massive duffel bag hangs from his shoulder.

He waves and winks.

Lexi hops off the wall.

"Ready?" he says, helping me down.

I nod and look at Lexi. "You're coming with us, right?"

"Sure."

Jax folds my hand into his while we start walking to the parking lot.

"If you win tomorrow, are you going to buy us all dinner with your prize money?" Lexi teases.

I snort, because no. If I win, every single cent of that one thousand dollars is going straight into my non-existent rainy day fund for the next time my car dies. Apartments in Lansing aren't cheap, and there won't be any closets to sleep in if something goes wrong.

My feet stumble. Jax holds me steady. "You OK?"

I nod, but my stomach clenches again. I haven't thought about Lansing in days. It used to be the brightest part of my day— thinking about moving. Now the thought just makes me lonely.

We're nearly to the end of the parking lot when we hear someone call Jax's name. A guy in a nondescript golf shirt and mirrored sunglasses approaches us carrying a messenger bag that looks like it has been dragged around the bases. My stomach drops like a rock. He has *scout* written all over him.

The Adam's apple bobs in Jax's throat bobs as he steps forward. "Can I help you?"

The man closes the distance between us, hand extended. Jax lets go of mine to accept it.

"Mike Morgan with the Washington Nationals. Got a minute?"

I look up at Jax. His expression has gone strangely blank. "I, um, do you want me to wait for you across the street?"

He barely blinks. "Sure."

Lexi grabs my elbow. "Awesome. See you over there."

My feet feel like lead as she pulls me along. "It probably doesn't mean anything," she says, voice laced with forced optimism. "He probably talks to scouts all the time."

Probably.

Because he's still a prospect.

And after weeks of living in a blissful bubble, I suddenly feel the approaching draft like a giant clock ticking toward midnight.

21

JAX

I watch Bree walk away, her gait stiff.

The scout clears his throat. "This a bad time?"

I look back at the man. "Sorry. No. What can I do for you?"

"Cut to the chase, huh? I can appreciate that."

I cross my arms.

"How's the shoulder?" he asks.

"Good as new." The automatic answer is getting old.

The scout nods. "Your pop time looks good. You're hitting big. You're agile. You look like your former self."

My former self? Physically, yeah. But in every other way? Not even close. I look back at Bree again. "Look, Mr. Morgan," I say, turning back around. "I don't mean to be disrespectful, but what exactly do you want?"

The man tilts his head. "You know, most guys this time of year trip over their own dicks trying to get my attention. You act like you couldn't care less."

"I do care. I just ..." I shrug. "I'm also not some naive high school kid who gets a hard-on every time a scout wants to talk to them."

"Is it serious? You and the girl?"

"How's that your business?"

"We evaluate everything, including the intangibles."

"Having a serious girlfriend is an intangible?"

"It can be."

"A good one or a bad one?"

"You tell me."

I shake my head. Everyone's a product to be measured. Even girlfriends. "I think she's the best thing that ever happened to me. That intangible enough for you?"

"That depends."

"On what?"

"On whether she's your priority or baseball is."

I scrub my hand over my mouth and jaw to hold back the things I want to say to this asshole. "We done here? Because I don't need to put up with this for some twenty-odd bid."

The guy laughs. "Shit, kid. You haven't been paying any fucking attention at all, have you? There were rumors, but shit. It's true."

"What kind of fucking rumors?"

"That you've basically gone into hiding, avoiding the press and shit."

"What's your point?"

The guy digs out his phone and types with his thumbs. Then he turns the phone around. "You're back on top."

My eyes focus on the screen, but I have to blink a few times to understand what I'm seeing. I grab the guy's phone. It's an app for a website I've come to despise called DraftDogs that reports exclusively on MLB draft prospects. I see my own picture under a headline from a half hour ago.

Tanner likely to go high after solid summer performance

The guy takes back his phone and shoves it in his pocket. "Maybe you haven't been paying attention to us, but we've been paying attention to you. So, get your shit together and make some choices."

I can barely get my voice to work. "What kind of choices?"

The guy manages to look almost sympathetic. "I'm sure you can figure it out."

The guy walks away, and I tear my gaze to Bree. She and Lexi sit at an outdoor patio table at the ice cream shop across the street. She looks over under the weight of my gaze. I hold up my hand and motion that I need a minute. She nods, a worried expression crossing her face.

I dig out my phone and realize I never turned it back on after the game. I power it up, and my screen explodes with messages from my parents. They must've seen the article.

Dad answers, voice tense. "I've been trying to call you."

"I know. I'm sorry." I scrub a hand over my hair. "You saw the article."

"Screw the article. Coach Brady's been trying to reach you."

I'm immediately on alert. "Why?"

"He's gotten four calls today."

My breathing stalls. When they start calling your college coach this close to the draft, it's serious. "Which teams?"

"Tampa Bay, Baltimore, Atlanta, and Vegas."

The Vegas Aces? Holy shit. That's my dream-come-true team.

My hands start to shake as Dad continues. "We have to get an agent lined up. You still like Manny Wolfe best?"

I drop my duffel bag, legs shaking. An agent. Holy shit. "Dad," I say, because it's all I can get out.

"I know, son. I know. It's happening. Do you want us to drive up there?"

"No."

"Afraid of jinxing it?"

I manage a laugh. "Yeah."

"Take a deep breath. This is what you've worked for your entire life."

"I know."

"Good. Now keep your focus. Just one more week."

I end the call, shove my phone back in my pocket, and scrub my hands up and down my face. My heart is pounding out of my chest. I finally turn back toward the ice cream shop. Bree is still watching me, wary.

I need to get her home. We've put this off long enough.

22

BREE

"THIS IS SO INCREDIBLE, JAX."

I'm perched stiffly on the edge of his bed, knees pinched together and hands knitted in my lap. My lips are frozen in a smile for his benefit.

My brain tries to catch up to everything he just told me—something about calls from teams, and his father lining up an agent, and he really needs to focus this week, and it's happening, it's finally happening for him, and holy shit, Bree, this is everything he's ever wanted, everything he thought he lost because of his injury.

I'm happy for him. Truly. This is what he deserves. But I also know.

This is how it ends for us.

This is how it was always going to end for us.

I rise on shaky legs. "I should probably—" I wave my hand toward the bathroom. "I should probably get all my stuff together."

Jax grips my elbow. "What? Why?"

"You need to focus. I don't want to get in the way of that. I'll make up a story and see if Lexi can put me up for a while."

"Hey," he says, gently. He tugs me back, and I walk into his embrace. "None of this means you have to leave, Bree."

"You're going to get drafted next week. I'll need to find a new place to stay then, anyway. It's probably just easier this way."

"Easier for who?"

I try to pull away, but he tightens his arms around me.

"I know what you're doing," he murmurs.

"I'm not doing anything. I'm trying to give you the space you need to focus."

He drops his mouth close to my ear. "I'm not your father, Bree. I'm not leaving you."

Cold. My whole body goes cold. "What are you talking about?"

"I know the truth about Brett. That he's not your stepfather."

"Have people been gossiping about me to you?"

"No," he says cautiously. Which means *yes*.

I yank away from his embrace. He tries to hold me back. "Bree—"

"Let me guess. Someone saw us together and gave you the whole dirty story, right? Warned you to stay away from me, right?"

"No one was gossiping about you," he says, voice low and gentle as if he expects my head to spin around. "My coach made an off-handed comment before the game today. That's it."

"What did he say?"

"It doesn't matter. I want to hear it from you."

Jax settles his hand on my arm just above the elbow, and for some reason, the gesture brings a lump to my throat.

"Don't run away again. Please."

Resignation steals my resolve. There's no point in hiding now. I lift my shoulder in a weak shrug. "It's just easier to say stepfather. I stopped thinking of him as my dad when I was a junior in high school."

Jax rubs his thumb across my elbow. "What happened your junior year?"

I shrug again, as if none of this matters anymore. "He left. He got a job as a supervisor for a corporate farm, and they needed him to go to Florida for the winter. I didn't want to leave my friends. So, he went without me."

"Who took care of you?"

"Nobody. He left me alone. Told me not to tell anyone, or we'd both get in trouble."

"Jesus, Bree." And there it is. Pity. "What happened?"

I square my shoulders to hide how much I want to shrink into myself. "A teacher finally figured it out and called child protective services. They were going to send me to live with a foster family, but Lexi's mom took me in. Brett was arrested for neglect."

"Did he go to jail?"

"No. He plead down to a misdemeanor, but he lost his job, and he blamed me for it." I swallow against the lump in my throat. "He was never a good father. He drank and couldn't keep a job. He wasn't exactly ready to be a father when my mom got pregnant. They never got married. I think he always resented me for tying him down."

I sneak a glance at Jax's face. His eyes are pinched at the corners, and his lips are pressed together in a thin line. I hate that look. I've seen it on too many faces in my life. I never wanted to see it on his.

Jax's arms come around me again. "I didn't know, Bree. Jesus, I didn't know."

I stiffen. "I don't need you to feel sorry for me."

"I don't," he says, pressing his forehead to my hair. "I hurt for you. Don't you know the difference?"

No. I don't.

He rests his chin on my head. "What happened at your graduation?"

"He didn't show up for the ceremony. I was still living with Lexi, so I'm not sure why I thought he would, but, you know, it was my big day and all."

"You *hoped* he would show up."

I nod. "Anyway, when he didn't, I decided to confront him. I drove out to his house. He was drunk. He gave me an old suitcase and told me pack the rest of my shit. He said I was officially an adult now, and his responsibility was officially over, and that was that. I haven't spoken to him since. Last I heard, he really did move to Florida."

Jax shifts, and his forehead comes down on mine. "I wish I'd known that night, Bree. Why didn't you tell me? I would have—"

I turn my face away. "You would have felt sorry for me and never touched me."

"That's not true."

"It's already true," I snap. "I'm not just *Bree* to you anymore. I'm Bree with the pathetic fucking childhood."

"Look at me."

I can't. I can't stand for him to look at me with the same pity that I see in everyone else's eyes.

"Hey," he urges quietly.

I finally meet his gaze. Sympathy radiates off him. I hate it. "If you're going to look at me like that, I'm going to sleep in my car."

He drops his forehead to mine again. "Bree, stop running away from me."

"I'm not running. You're leaving."

"But I'm not leaving *you*."

My lips part as the air starts to seep from my lungs. He's so dangerously close to breaking through my walls that I want to squeeze my eyes shut. My body begins to tremble. I turn my head again, but he cradles my face in his hands.

His thumbs caress my jaw. "When was the last time someone told you they love you?"

23

JAX

HER SILENCE IS MY ANSWER.

"You can't remember, can you?"

"No." She trembles in my hands.

Pain stabs clear through me. I've been told how much I'm loved every day of my life for as long as I can remember. Multiple times a day from my parents and my grandparents and, yeah, even my siblings when they're not being little assholes. Christ, even my coach hugged me before I went in to surgery and said, "I love you, kid."

I've heard, "I love you," so many times in my life that the words almost lost their meaning.

Not anymore. New, deeper understanding explodes in my chest until my already battered heart shreds. I don't just hear the words in my mind. For the first time in my life, I feel them.

Urgent emotion presses against the back of my throat, so I

squeeze my eyes shut to hold it back. But I can't hide the shake of my chest as I draw in a breath or the whimper of sound that emerges when I let it out.

I open my eyes and weave my fingers into her hair. "That ends today."

She whimpers as I mold my mouth to hers.

I kiss down her throat and back up again until I reach her lips once more. "Bree McTavish ..."

I drop a whisper of a kiss on her lips. Her breathing starts again, fast and hard.

"I—" Another kiss, a little longer this time.

"Jax Tanner." I brush her lips again, and she begins to tremble.

"Love you."

And then I claim her mouth fully, fiercely. I pour all that pent-up emotion into my kiss. I back her up to the bed and coax her onto it. Then I lace our hands together and slide them over her head. My body throbs with a need to be inside her, to claim her and comfort her and make her cry out with the joy of pleasure. The joy of being loved.

We shed our clothes, and all I can think as we move together, one body, one soul, is that this is what it feels like when it's real. This desperation. This primal need. This certainty.

We don't speak, because we don't need to. She's telling me feels the same with the tender caress of her fingertips up and down my spine. She speaks to me with a turn of her face, a press of her lips on the scar along my shoulder. She confesses her feelings with a sob of a sound that sends her arching into me, her head tilted back, her breaths a frantic pant.

I press my hands into the mattress and steady myself to go deeper, harder. The bed creaks and groans with every thrust of my hips.

"Jax," she moans.

I drop my forehead to hers and try to ignore the shiver up my spine, the tightening in my groin. Not yet. Not yet. Not until she reaches her release.

She cries out and arches again. Her legs tighten around me, and I'm done. I bury myself deeper into her passion and let it carry me over the edge with her. I cry her name and shudder as every part of me explodes in a blinding burst of pleasure that is better than before, better than anything I've ever known.

My elbows shake, and I collapse on top of her. She immediately wraps her arms around my back and holds me there. Our labored breathing is the only sound in the room.

"Jax," she murmurs a moment later.

"Yeah?"

I almost don't trust my ears when I hear her quiet voice. "I love you, too."

Don't cry. Don't fucking cry. I clear my throat. "It's the beard, isn't it?"

Her laughter fixes all the broken pieces of me.

I don't want to hide from my future anymore. I want to sprint as fast as I can into it.

With her.

24

BREE

THE DAY of the contest starts early, when dawn is still just a yellow promise on the horizon and a hazy mist hangs over the lake. Jax skips his morning run to help me haul my stuff over to the fairgrounds.

It's a big week for both of us, because the draft is tomorrow. The past several days have been a blur of games, contest prep, press speculation about Jax's prospects, and unrelenting nerves. But our nights always end the same—wrapped up in each other. Together.

Jax kills the engine in front of the massive on-site food center where each contestant will prepare their entries during an assigned kitchen time. Mine isn't until noon, but we're all required to check in with our supplies at seven o'clock. Which leaves me way too much time to gnaw on my nails.

"Nervous?"

"No," I respond. "Yes. I don't know. I'm up against professional chefs."

"Stop worrying," Jax chides gently, leaning across the console to tug me close for a kiss. "If you don't win, it's because the judges have no taste buds."

"You're biased."

"True." He kisses me again. "I'm sorry I can't be here."

"Don't be. You have a game. And you'll be here tonight when they announce the winners. That's enough."

He kisses me softly. "I'm going to enjoy celebrating when you win."

A hot flush creeps up my body. "Got something special in mind?"

"I'm thinking whipped cream and chocolate sauce might be involved."

"You're taking me out for ice cream?"

He laughs. "Let's get this stuff inside."

It takes a half hour to get me checked in and to store my things. Afterward, I walk him back to his car. He leans against the driver's side door and tugs me close. "What time are Lexi and her mom getting here?"

We're allowed two assistants. "Just before noon."

"You sure you want to hang out here until then? I can bring you back to the house for a while."

"No, I like it here. I'll go feed the goats at the petting zoo or something. I'd go crazy sitting around the house."

He leans in to kiss me goodbye, but his phone rings and interrupts him. He digs it from his pocket and checks the screen. "It's my dad."

I step back as he answers, but he keeps his hand laced with mine, his thumb tracing a lazy circle against my palm.

His eyes widen. "When?"

I can't tell if it's good news or bad. "What's wrong?" I whisper.

He shakes his head. Listens some more. Then, "I need to call you back. Give me five minutes."

He ends the call, and I don't even have time to ask him what's going on. He lets out a loud whoop and grabs me to spin me around.

"Oh my God," I laugh. "What is happening?"

"Two scouts from the Aces want to meet with me tonight," he says, setting me down.

"That's your dream team!"

"I know." Jax plants his hands on his head. "I can't believe it. Holy shit."

"What time tonight?"

"I don't know." He cups my face in his hands. "But I swear, I will be here for the announcement at six. I swear."

"It's OK—"

He cuts me off with a kiss, hard and fast, and then sets me back. Digging his keys from the pocket of his shorts, he climbs into his truck. I retreat a step as he starts the engine.

"Hey," he says, leaning from the open door with arm outstretched. I take his hand and let him tug me close.

"I love you," he says before lowering his mouth to mine again, this time softer. A series of small, playful kisses follows before he finally pulls back with a smile that reminds me of a golden retriever with a new bone.

Or a naughty ball of white fluff with a stolen bra.

"I love you, too," I say, kissing him one more time.

I wave as he drives away, but he's already on the phone.

25

JAX

DAD ANSWERS IMMEDIATELY.

"What time do they want to meet me?"

"Five-thirty."

Fuck. I clench the steering wheel. "Can they do it earlier?"

"Do you have something better to do?"

I glance in the rearview mirror. Bree still stands where I left her. "I, yeah, sort of."

"OK. That's interesting. Do you want to fill me in?"

Heat rises on my neck. "I have a, um, a ... "

Dad laughs. "What's her name?"

"Bree," I exhale.

Dad laughs again, louder this time. "You finally made that happen, huh? No wonder you never call home."

"Look, she has something really important tonight at six."

"More important than a meeting with two scouts from the team you've dreamed of signing with since you were in eighth grade?"

"Dad—"

"Do you know how unusual this is for them to meet with you this close to the draft?"

"I know, but—"

"But what? I know how much you've always liked this girl, but you've been dating, what, three weeks? At the most? That hardly seems long enough to risk your shot with the Aces."

I opt against pointing out that he proposed to Mom just a month after they started dating, a story my siblings and I have been forced to hear every year on their anniversary.

"You don't understand, Dad. She—" How do I explain without giving my parents the wrong impression of her or without going into the whole damn story and betraying her privacy? But dammit! I feel like I'm being forced to choose between the game I love and the girl I love.

"Son, listen to me. You've worked your entire life for this. Right now, this is the most important thing in the world to you. Get your head in the game."

"Dad—"

"She will understand, Jackson, if she's the right girl for you."

She *is*. But Dad's right. I can't risk screwing up my chance with the Vegas Aces. "Schedule the meeting."

Bree will understand. Right? She has to.

So why do I wait until I know she can't answer the phone to call and tell her I won't be there tonight?

26

BREE

THE NOISE of clanging dishes and too many voices inside the food center makes it hard to hear Jax's voicemail, but I make out the important part.

He's not going to make it tonight.

It would be a lie to say I'm not disappointed, but of course the meeting with the Aces has to come first.

I return my phone to my purse and turn back to the long counter where fair-goers taste samples of my barbecue sauce and roasted morels. Lexi ran to the bathroom a few minutes ago, leaving me alone with Missy, her mom.

Missy smiles as she replenishes a tray of beef tips. "I think this is everyone's favorite. You'll have to be sure to put this on the menu of your restaurant."

Warmth spreads through my chest, chasing away the chill left from Jax's voicemail. Missy has always believed in me. I close the short distance between us and give her a quick hug.

"What's this for?" she laughs.

"For everything. Thank you for helping me today. For always helping me."

"Aw, sweetie." Missy hugs me tighter. "You don't have to thank me. We're family."

Tears sting my eyes. I cough self-consciously and pull away to find hers glimmering with wetness, too. Together, we laugh and wipe away the emotion.

I study her for a moment—the face that looks so much like Lexi's, the long dark hair that is always piled high in a bun, the tiny laugh lines around her eyes. I try to picture her twenty years younger, falling in love with a Slugger, pregnant with his child, and then abandoned.

"Can I ask you something?"

Her smile grows. "Anything."

"Lexi's father … " I clear my throat. "What happened?"

Weariness drains the smile from her face. She leans against the counter. "He left."

"Did he know you were pregnant?"

"Honestly? I don't know. I tried to tell him, but he wouldn't even take my calls. I left messages. He just never returned them. Eventually, I just gave up trying. He made it clear with his silence he didn't want me or the baby."

"Were you in love with him?"

"I thought so. I even thought he loved me. But—" She shrugs. "I guess I was wrong."

"How come you've never told Lexi who he is?"

"I offered to tell her when she turned eighteen. She said she didn't care."

That's news to me. I guess Lexi has secrets, too.

Missy tilts her head. "Why are you asking?"

I shrug. "I don't know."

"I think you do."

I avoid her eyes. She takes my hand. "From what Lexi has told me, it's different with you and Jax. But I'd be a bad mother if I didn't at least give you some advice." Her fingers squeeze mine. "The one thing I've learned from my own experience and from watching other girls year after year is that there is one thing these guys love more than anything else in the world, and that's baseball. Nothing is as important to them as the game. And they resent anything and anyone that gets in the way."

My chest caves in on itself. "That was him on my voicemail. He can't come tonight. He has a meeting with the Aces."

Missy's sigh carries an unspoken *I told you so.* "Maybe he's different, Bree. I hope he's different. But I know you and what you've been through and how hard you've worked. You deserve to be the most important thing in the world to someone."

27

JAX

BEE HASN'T CALLED BACK by the time I walk into the old, dusty conference room in the Long Ballers clubhouse, but I don't have time to worry about it.

Two men greet me. I recognize them as Juan Duarte and Brad Whitney—Aces scouts who have been at my Ohio State games. I sit and try to stop my knee from bouncing up and down.

"We need to get a couple of things out in the open right up front," Juan says. "First, this meeting is unusual. We don't normally do these kinds of sit-downs. Second, we're not allowed to tell you which round we're considering you for, only which round you may have been evaluated for. Understand?"

Yeah. I know the rules. "But you *are* considering me."

"We wouldn't meet with you if we weren't," Brad says.

My knee starts to shake again.

Juan lays his forearms on the table and leans. "We're not going to beat around the bush. You're looking good. Real good. But I'm sure you know there are other things we evaluate besides performance on the field."

"Intangibles."

"Right," Brad says. "There's talent. And there's commitment. You have the first, no doubt. We need to gauge where you are on the second."

I blink, and sweat prickles under my arms. "What do you mean, sir?"

Brad crosses his arms. "How badly do you want to sign with a Major League ball club?"

The sweat begins to pool. "More than anything I've ever wanted in my life."

Juan sits back in his chair. "Rumor has it that you have a serious girlfriend."

"Is that important?"

"It can be. This is a hard life for the WAGs."

WAGs. As in wives and girlfriends. "I know, sir."

"It takes a strong girl to put up with the travel, the stress of long absences and trade deadlines, the press. The wrong girl can make life hell on a player. You sure she's ready for it?"

"Yes," I say automatically, but doubt has wiggled its way inside. *Is* she ready for it?

"So, if you were offered a contract, you would sign?" Juan asks.

My heart pounds. "Absolutely."

"And if the phone rang, you'd answer it?"

Oh my God. "In an instant."

The scouts stare at me, and I try not to squirm.

"Any questions for us?" Brad says.

"Is my phone going to ring?"

Brad's eyebrows shoot high on his forehead. "We set up a sit-down meeting with you. You have to ask?"

"Yes. Which night?"

Brad laughs. I can't tell if that's good or bad.

"You can tell me that without revealing a specific round," I say.

Brad and Juan exchange a look. Juan shrugs. "Keep your phone on *tomorrow*."

Holy shit.

That's when they announce the first and second round draft picks.

They want me in the first or second round. Holy shit. I'm back. I'm really back.

My head spins. My mouth goes dry.

The men rise and extend their hands. I rise and shake both. "Thank you for the meeting," I somehow manage to say.

My legs are still shaky when I walk out. I pull out my phone to see if Bree has called back yet. She hasn't. But the awards ceremony hasn't started yet. If I drive fast, I can make it before it's over.

I grab my stuff from the locker room and jog out to the car.

I realize as soon as I pull out, driving fast is not going to be an option. The festival grounds are on the other side of town, and it seems like every single person in Silver Lake is heading there. It takes twenty minutes just to make it through traffic and another ten to get into the parking lot. And once there, I have to circle a thousand times to find a spot.

I text her to let her know I'm coming, but she doesn't respond.

I jog all the way—darting around families and dogs, past food vendors and carnival rides. My phone rings, and I yank it from my pocket.

"Bree?"

My dad laughs. "Uh, no. What happened at the meeting?"

I stop and plant a hand on my head. "They told me to keep my phone on tomorrow night."

I wait for it to sink in. "Holy shit, Jax."

"I gotta go. I'll call you later, OK?"

"What? Jax, we have stuff we need to talk about!"

I end the call and start running again. My stomach sinks as I hear a woman talking on the stage, thanking everyone for coming and for all the people who entered.

Fuck. Please God, tell me I didn't miss it.

The stage comes into view. I scan the crowd. I spot Mrs. C and Lexi first. Then, finally, standing apart from them, I see Bree. She's talking to a tall man in a dark suit.

I start to jog toward her, but Lexi suddenly grabs my arm.

"Hold up, cowboy," she says.

"What happened?" I pant.

"You missed it," she says.

Fuck. I plant my hands on my head. "And?"

Lexi cocks an eyebrow. "And she won."

I feel a grin all the way from my chest. I start toward Bree again, but Lexi holds me back. Again. "Uh, not right now."

"Who is that?" I ask, pointing to the man she's talking to.

"Don't you watch TV?"

"Not really."

"Dirk Vacho. He was the celebrity judge. He's the head of culinary services for the Beckinsale hotel chain."

"Holy shit. Are you serious? What's he talking to her about?"

Lexi shrugs, and I swear her smile seems sinister. "No idea," she says. "But it kind of looks like she's being scouted, doesn't it?"

28

BREE

"ARE YOU SERIOUS?"

Mr. Vacho smiles and hands me his card. "I can see you're shocked, and I know it's a lot to take in at once. But I leave tomorrow, so I wanted to talk to you as soon as possible."

My eyes trail down to the card in my hand, clutched together with the winning thousand-dollar check. My brain is sluggish, trying to catch up. It was shocking enough to win. Now this?

"I don't—" I swallow. "I need to make sure I understand. You're offering me a chance to apply to the Beckinsale Culinary Arts Institute?"

He smiles again. "No. I'm offering you a spot in the institute. No application. It's yours. We have a new cohort starting in three weeks, and you could choose among several locations to start— Nashville, Miami, Boston, or Las Vegas. You rotate every six months for two years, and then you apprentice at one of our major hotels for another year."

I feel faint. Oh my God. How is this happening? Stuff like this doesn't happen to me. "I don't understand. How can you just accept me on a whim?"

"Why do you think I agree to do contests like this? I'm scouting for talent. And trust me, your talent will be wasted at a community college program."

"Mr. Vacho, that's an amazing offer, and I really appreciate it, but there's no way I can afford—"

He holds up his hand. "I know what you're going to say. We have scholarships and other financial aid options to cover tuition, housing, and supplies. Plus, you get paid for any hours worked in the kitchens after your initial classes. Don't let money stop you from accepting the offer."

Mr. Vacho looks at his watch. "Look, I have to run. My cell number is on the back of the card. I know it's short notice, but I will need a decision by Saturday so I can get you enrolled. Call me as soon as you decide."

He takes a step but then stops and looks back. "An opportunity like this won't come your way again, Bree. All you have to do is say yes."

The world crawls to a halt. I've just been handed a ready-made dream come true. A month ago, I was sleeping in a closet. Now I have the opportunity of a lifetime staring me in the face. My own fairy tale ending.

So why do I feel like my heart is breaking?

Because Jax isn't here. My disappointment is childish, selfish. Of course the meeting had to come first. But Missy's words won't let me go.

They resent anything and anyone who gets in the way.

You deserve to be the most important thing in the world to someone.

And then it's not Missy's voice I hear.

I could've been something, but I'm stuck here because your mother got pregnant.

Take your shit and get out. You're an adult now, and I'm done. I'm taking my life back.

So am I. "Mr. Vacho."

He turns around.

"Yes."

29

JAX

SOMETHING'S WRONG.

Bree walks toward Lexi, Mrs. C and me with a wooden gait, a blank expression, like a statue. She can't go a step without someone stopping her to offer congratulations, but she doesn't look like someone who just won a big contest and a thousand bucks.

She looks like someone whose father just tossed her out with a suitcase.

I push through the crowd with Lexi and Mrs. C until we finally reach Bree. Lexi screams something unintelligible and squeezes Bree in a tight hug. Mrs. C pushes Lexi aside and takes her turn. When I finally wrap my arms around her, though, she's stiff.

I lower my mouth to her ear so only she can hear me. "Babe, I'm so sorry I missed it. But I have some amazing news."

Bree pulls away from my embrace. "So do I."

A twinge of alarm jolts my muscles. "What did that guy say to you?"

Her lips curl into a fake smile. "He, uh ..." She looks at Lexi and Mrs. C, but not me. She looks everywhere but at me. "He offered me a spot in the Beckinsale Culinary Arts Institute."

Lexi lets out another scream, and Mrs. C starts praising the Lord.

I alone seem to be slow on the uptake. "Wow. That's ... wow." I run my hand over my hair. "That's amazing, Bree. What exactly does that mean?"

She still won't look at me. "It means I would get to train with some of the top chefs in the country. No community college. No more saving money. It's everything I ever wanted."

Everything I ever wanted. A chill races through me.

Mrs. C yanks her into another hug. "My girl. My girl. I'm so proud of you."

This is a good thing. I'm supposed to be happy for her, right? So why does my heart feel like it wants to crawl out of my chest? "When do you have to decide?"

Mrs. C scoffs. "What's there to decide?"

A lot. I close the distance between us. "Bree."

She swallows and look up.

"What did you tell him?" I ask in a voice I barely recognize.

"Jax, we need to talk."

THERE ARE words coming from her mouth. I hear them, but I can't understand them because my brain is moving about as fast as the decrepit horses in the pony rides behind us.

We're alone in an alley between a corn dog cart and an

elephant ears vendor. Mrs. C and Lexi hover nearby to stand guard and pretend they're not listening.

"Wait, just wait." I drag my hands over my hair. "Just start at the beginning. So, this means you have to move? Like, out of Michigan?"

She nods. "I would start in one city and rotate every six months."

So, it's basically the minor leagues. Which means both of us will be moving around a lot for a while. It's OK. We can make it work. Maybe she can wait to select a city until I find out where I'm going.

I pull her against me and tuck her face into the crook of my shoulder. "I'm so proud of you, babe."

She's cold and stiff in my arms.

"Bree?"

She sighs and pulls away. The shimmer of tears in her eyes sends a shiver down my spine.

"Bree, what's wrong?"

"Jax, I just think, I mean, maybe we need to—" She looks away, and a loud buzzing in my ears drowns out all other noise.

I got hit in the head once by a fastball behind the plate. It flipped off the end of a bat and wham! It bounced against the ear flap of my helmet and sent me sprawling on my back with my eyes dancing.

This feels a lot like that.

"Oh my God," I exhale. "You're running away from me again."

"I'm not." Her lip trembles. "I just think maybe we need to slow down, take some time to get settled and, you know, make sure."

"I'm already sure."

"You think so now, but what about in a few months?"

"I'll still love you!" My heart screeches to a halt as I'm gripped with a new fear. "But maybe you don't really love me."

Her voice shakes. "I do, Jax."

I bend to plant my hands on my thighs. But then I stand again almost immediately with a delirious laugh, because Christ, we've gone back in time. We're back in the pantry, and she's shoving stuff in a bag as fast as she can and darting into the rain to get away from me because ... Christ. Of all the ironies. Most guys have to worry about groupies who are only interested in the money and fame. I fall in love with the one girl who wants none of it.

"I'm still just a fucking *prospect* to you," I growl. "That's it, isn't it? You only wanted me when my career was going nowhere."

"That's not true," she says, inching toward me. "I love you."

"Then what is this?"

She shakes her head. A tear escapes her eye and journeys down her cheek. It tears a hole in my heart.

I reach for her, and this time, thank God, she lets me pull her closer. "Babe, talk to me. Is this because I missed tonight? I told you I'm sorry. I feel terrible about it."

"*That's* why!" She tugs from my grip of her elbows. "You feel guilty. And it's going to happen again. You're going to have to put baseball first, and someday, that guilt is going to turn to resentment, and, I can't ..."

I can barely talk. "Can't what?"

"I don't have your perfect life to fall back on if this thing falls apart."

"Bullshit," I growl, cutting her off, because my heart is bleeding out, and all I have left is anger. "This has nothing to do with me and my life. This is *your* issue."

Tears fall freely down her face. It takes all my willpower to not yank her to me and wipe them away. But I can't do it. I can't do it anymore.

"You know what, Bree? I *do* feel sorry for you. We have something real, but you're going to throw it away because you'd rather keep dragging around your father's shitty, little suitcase than take the risk of staying. And until you're willing to let that go, you're going to be running from people your entire life."

Bile stings the back of my throat as I whip around to leave.

Beg me to stay, baby. Please.

"Jax."

I spin back around, heart pounding with hope.

But then it sinks. Because she's not looking at me like she's going to beg me to stay. She looks at me like *she* feels sorry for *me*.

"You're right. But at least I acknowledge my suitcase."

"What the hell does that mean?"

"There was a reason you wanted to hide from the world for a while with me," she says, voice wobbly. "But I can't solve your fear of failing. Only you can do that."

My stomach revolts. I don't need to hear this shit. "I'll leave your stuff in the pantry, Cinderella. Have a nice life."

I MAKE it all the way to my car before throwing up. I lean on the door and purge myself of all the anger, fear, and adrenaline coursing through me until there's nothing left. I can't believe this is happening. I can't believe she's leaving me.

"Wow."

I whip around, wiping my mouth. Lexi stands next to the car wearing an ugly grimace. My heart skips as my eyes automatically search for Bree. But, of course, she's not there. Why would she be? She's fucking leaving me.

"Mrs. C took her home," Lexi supplies. "And since my mom already left—thank God, because she would castrate you if she saw that—looks like you get to do the honors for me."

Fuuuck. I swipe my hand over my face. "Lexi, can't you call someone?"

"Nope." She rounds the front of my car to the passenger side. "And by the way, I thought I'd seen all the worst ways a guy could screw up with a girl, but that was a Major League fuck-up right there."

"She's the one who's running away."

Lexi snorts and looks at me like I just gave a stupid answer in class. "Yeah, keep telling yourself that, bro."

Christ. I unlock the car and slide behind the wheel.

"I don't know where you live," I grumble as I pull out. I can't fucking believe I'm driving her home right now instead of crawling to the nearest bar and drowning myself in whiskey.

"I'll direct you." She digs around in her purse and hands me a mint.

I glower but accept it, because that is some nasty shit going on in my mouth right now.

"This is my fault," Lexi says, settling into her seat.

"What?"

"I'm the one who told Bree to go for it with you. I thought, *what the hell?* You're hot. She needed a taste of something savory for a change, and you're like fresh-from-the garden asparagus. All hard and stiff and—"

I whip my gaze away from the road. "What the fuck, Lexi?"

"Never mind. The point is, I hate baseball players. Always have. I think you're all a bunch of selfish, alpha-male assholes who don't care about anything but scoring, and I don't just mean at home plate."

"You have the right to remain silent, you know."

"The thing is, you're not like that."

"Gee, thanks."

"You're worse."

"Excuse me?"

"You're the opposite of an asshole alpha-male. You're like a, a —" She looks around as if searching for the right word. "You're like one of those dogs they bring into hospitals. You know those therapy dogs? That's you. You're a sucker for sadness. You walk into a room, find the loneliest person there, and immediately shove your face in their armpit."

I'd laugh if I weren't on the verge of collapsing into a ball of hysterical sobbing. And, I realize with a sickening swallow, if it weren't the most accurate description of me ever. *I'm* going to fucking need a therapy dog after tonight.

"But the thing that's really bugging me right now is that I'm afraid that's all you see about her."

The hair on my arms rises with goose bumps. I don't like where she's going with this.

"You just called her Cinderella. That's how you see her, don't you?"

"No," I growl.

"You do. Because you're Prince Therapy Dog who's so busy trying to save her from that shitty, little suitcase that you can't appreciate all the things inside it."

"That's bullshit. I love her." Oh my God. I love her, and I've lost her, and I'm going to fucking die right here in the car.

"Turn left at the light," Lexi says. Then, "Why do you love her?"

"What kind of fucking question is that?"

"Turn right. Third house on the left. And forget I asked. I'm not the one who needs to hear the answer, anyway."

I pull into the driveway and stare straight ahead. "How long did she live here with you?"

"Almost two years."

My throat closes.

A light goes on over the front door, and a woman walks out who looks like a slightly older version of Lexi.

Lexi opens her window and leans out it. "It's just me, Mom. I'm with Jax, and he just broke up with Bree—"

"She broke up with me!"

"—and I'm going to read him the riot act now. I'll come in in a few minutes and tell you everything."

Lexi's mom looks in my general direction with an expression that either means she feels sorry for what's coming to me or wants to contribute to it. Then she goes back inside. Lexi closes the window and faces me in the dark.

I scrub my hand over my jaw. "Lexi, whatever you want to say to me, save it, because—"

"Shut up."

I snap my mouth shut.

"She panicked, Jax. That's what she does."

"Really? Well, I can't spend my entire life worrying she's going to panic every time I get traded or something goes wrong. Baseball is a cruel world with no certainties. I've spent the past six months learning that the hard way."

Lexi tilts her head. "Six whole months? Wow. How horrible."

My skin gets hot.

"Did you ever tell her you were in this for the long haul?"

"I told her I love her."

"But did you ever say, *Bree, I love you and want you to be with you forever?*"

"Isn't that assumed when you love someone?"

"Isn't it assumed that a father will never abandon his daughter?"

My stomach starts to revolt again.

She makes a tsk sound. "Yep. There it is. You're starting to figure it out now, aren't you?"

Lexi turns in her seat to face me fully. "Love isn't a guarantee in her life. It never has been. And if you asked her what her greatest fear is, she'd say being abandoned, but that's not true. Her greatest fear is being resented. Becoming a burden on someone. And all you did tonight is reinforce that."

Bile rises in my throat.

"By the way," Lexi says, way too casually. "The *have a nice life* part was a nice touch. Did you do that on purpose?"

I can barely talk. "Why would I say that on purpose?"

"Because it's the last thing her father said to her."

I throw open my door.

And puke all over the driveway.

A hard hand bangs my back. "That's it. Let all that guilt and shame out. The raccoons will love it later."

I gag and sink back against my seat.

"Here comes the riot act," she says.

Wow. We haven't even gotten there yet?

"Don't even fucking think about talking to her again until you figure out what's in your own damn suitcase. You might be carrying around more expensive luggage, but right now, it's full of a whole lotta nothing. And you don't deserve her."

She opens her door and gets out. She stops in the glare of my headlights to give me a too-sweet smile and a fake, girly wave. She quickly twists it into the finger. Then she storms off toward her front porch, leaving me alone with a gut-punching epiphany.

We didn't go back in time to the pantry.

We went all the way back to the beach. And I've fucked it up for good this time.

30

BREE

I'M NUMB.

"You OK, honey?" Mrs. C pats my knee.

I nod, thankful for the shadows in the car so she can't see the truth on my face. Because the truth is, I'm not OK. I'm breaking in two. What have I done?

Mrs. C pulls into the parking lot of Edsel House and turns off the car. I reach for the handle. "Thanks for the ride."

She shuts off the car. "I'm not done with you yet, young lady. Follow me."

I'm too weary to argue. I trudge behind her through the service entrance.

She marches through the dark kitchen to the basement door. It creaks as she pulls it open. A cold sweat breaks out under my arms. "Where are we going?"

"Just follow me."

I try to hold in my tears as we take the path I followed nearly every morning after I started sleeping in the pantry until the night I moved into Jax's room. I follow her down a dingy hallway that leads to the basement staircase. At the bottom she turns left. Toward the old servants' bedrooms.

She stops in front of one, unlocks it with a key on her massive ring, and opens the door. She stands aside then and motions for me to go in.

I hesitate. "What are we doing here?"

"Go in and see for yourself."

I sigh and walk into the dark room. At least this little excursion is giving me something to do besides panic and fall into a heap.

Mrs. C comes in behind me and flips the light switch. It takes a moment for my eyes to adjust to the dim lighting inside. But when they do, I spin around and gape at Mrs. C.

"What is this?"

"It's your bedroom. The one that Miss and I prepared for you back in April as soon as we figured out what you were doing."

"*Wh-what?*"

She snorts and walks in. "Did you really think no one would notice that you were suddenly hanging around the house until well past your shift ended? Or that I wouldn't see the giant black duffel bag behind one of the shelves in the pantry?"

Shame and embarrassment heat my cheeks. "Why didn't you say something? Or Missy?"

"Because we know you, girl. The only thing you hate more than asking for help is having someone know you need it."

Her description of me is so spot-on that I can only blink. She laughs. "What? You think I don't know that about you? You've worked for me for four years, Briana McTavish, and you're not as good at hiding stuff as you think you are."

"Did Lexi know?"

"Yep. We all agreed we weren't going to say anything until you asked for help."

I look around the room again, stopping at each piece of furniture—the bed covered by a pink-and-green quilt, a nightstand with a lamp, a dresser with a mirror above it. It's beautiful. I'm so overcome that all I can do is cover my mouth with my hand. I've never had a bedroom before. Not a real one. Not my own. I had to sleep on the couch growing up. And my apartment was a basic piece-of-crap studio.

Jax's room was never mine to begin with.

And just like that, I can't hold it inside any longer. I cover my face with my hands and cry.

Mrs. C wraps her arms around me and holds me. "That's it. Let all that ugly stuff out. All that stuff you keep bottled up."

I let myself sink into her. Let my head rest on her shoulder.

She rocks me. "I know you clam up whenever someone tries to get into any kind of feely, emotional stuff, but since you're crying anyway, I'm going to say something."

I sniffle.

Mrs. C pats my back. "I don't have any kids of my own. You and Lexi and the other girls are the closest thing to children I've ever had, and I care about all my girls. But if someone asked me who my favorite is, I would answer, without hesitation, *you*."

I cough.

"And it's not because you've had the roughest go of things, which you have. You drew the shortest damn stick in the bunch with your mom dying and getting stuck with that sonuvabitch as a sorry excuse for a father."

She takes a deep breath, and I think maybe she's going to cry, too. "The reason you're my favorite is because I've never, not once, seen you let it hold you back. You march on, no matter the setbacks. You have a plan, and you stick to it. But while that's your most admirable quality, it's also your greatest weakness, Bree."

That draws me back. Her expression is gentle in a way I've never seen from her before.

"Sometimes we cling to our plans because they're safe. Like a fast ball You always know you can hit it, because it comes at you straight down the middle. But sometimes you have to risking swinging at the curves, even if you might miss, because they make the best home runs."

She suddenly laughs. "Not bad for an old lady who hates baseball, huh?"

I wish I could laugh with her, but I can't. "I don't understand what you're saying."

"This Beckinsale thing is an amazing opportunity. I'm so proud of you. You deserve it. But you deserve to be happy in other ways, too."

My heart thuds as my throat gets thick.

"That boy loves you, Bree. He looks at you like the sun rises and sets in you alone."

A tear escapes down my cheek along with a sob-like sound. Not anymore. He's never going to look at me like that again.

Mrs. C holds my arms. "You never learned to trust people, Bree. I know that. But he's right. Until you learn how, you're always going to be afraid." She cups my face in her hands. "Take the risk, Bree."

She nods then and backs up. "There now. Get some rest. Take tomorrow off. Have yourself a good long cry. I'll come by in the morning with breakfast."

I sit down awkwardly on the bed. The mattress squeaks quietly.

Mrs. C kisses my forehead and walks out. She shuts the door behind her, leaving me alone with a sickening realization.

I've spent so much time worrying about people turning me away that I didn't appreciate all the people in my life who love me, who care about me, who will never, ever leave me.

Now I'm alone in a basement room with cold floors and no windows. Maybe I really am Cinderella.

Except I've broken my own glass slipper.

I crawl onto the bed, hug the pillow, and sob.

31

JAX

EVERYONE IS AVOIDING ME.

The rec room is a loud, chaotic party as we wait for the live broadcast of the draft to start. I should be surrounded by a crowd of guys patting me on the back, handing me beers, living their dreams vicariously through me while we wait for my phone to ring.

But I'm alone the couch. Because I'm a fucking bear who has growled at anyone who has come near me all day. I can barely function. Coach didn't even let me play today. He took one look at me and told the back-up catcher to warm up.

My phone rings in my pocket for the tenth time. It's my dad's ring tone again. He's been trying all day.

I ignore it. Again. He wants to talk about baseball, the draft, and I don't give a fuck.

I can't find her. Mrs. C won't tell me where she is. Neither will

Lexi. Her phone goes straight to voicemail. I even looked in the goddamned pantry.

The music for the start of the draft fills the room, and the guys get quiet. I feel the heavy weight of their stares. They're excited for me. Nervous for me. Scared of me.

But I'm numb.

I can't get her face out of my mind. Or her voice. *There was a reason you wanted to hide from the world for a while. But I can't solve your fear of failing.*

She's right. I'm terrified of failing, of losing.

Because my fucking suitcase is empty.

I've spent my whole life focused on nothing but baseball that I forgot to fill it up with other things, to appreciate everything else I have in my life. Including her. Lexi was right. I don't deserve Bree. I clung to her to fill up my empty spaces, to replace baseball.

But that's not how love works.

And now I've lost her.

My dad calls again.

I stand with a loud curse and stomp toward the terrace.

"Dude, where are you going?" Grady yells.

I yank open the terrace door and walk out, sucking in giant gulps of lake air. I dig my phone from my pocket and hit my dad's number.

He answers immediately. "Jesus fucking Christ, Jackson. Where have you been?"

And just like that, I break.

"Dad," I say, voice shaking as motherfucking tears form in my goddamned eyes.

Dad's tone changes in an instant. "What's wrong? What happened?"

"Bree…" I say, because it's all I can get out.

"What about Bree?"

I suck in another breath because I can't fucking get enough air into my lungs.

"Dammit, Jackson! What about Bree?"

"I—I fucked it up."

"Jax, the draft is on, and you're calling me about a girl?"

I manage a weird laugh. "Yeah."

He gets quiet. Heavy quiet. I hear him let out a long breath as if he's sitting down. "Wow." He lets out a small surprised laugh. "She's the real thing, isn't she?"

"Yeah." She was.

"I should've known. You're just like me. When I met your mother, I just knew. I gave you shitty advice yesterday, Jax. I'm sorry."

I walk to the balustrade and lean against it. The lake is dark and still in the distance.

"Jackson, talk to me."

"I need to ask you something," I say, trying to steady my voice.

"Anything."

"What if I don't make it?"

Dad's sigh is long and heavy. "Son, the fact that you think you have to ask me that right now tells me I've failed you a thousand different ways."

My throat is thick again. "No, you haven't."

"Your mom and I used to lie awake at night worried about you. Did you know that?"

"No. Why?"

"It's a scary thing to have a son who starts getting scouted in middle school. You want to encourage him to keep going and work hard and dream big, but you also want him to know it's OK if it doesn't work out. I've been good at the first part. But I have failed miserably at the second part."

"Dad—"

"You are my son, and I love you no matter what happens tonight. I love you if you never throw another goddamned ball in your life. I love you because you're smart and funny and kind. I love you because you make your sisters laugh, and you took the blame for your brother crashing the car in high school. Don't think I didn't know the truth about that one. I love you because you're you. And I cannot imagine how a man could be prouder of a son than I am."

I bend at the waist, rest my arm on the stone, and lay my forehead against it. Christ, I'm crying. I'm fucking crying.

"Tell me about your girl," he says.

I stand and turn my face into my shoulder to dry my cheeks. "She's smart and talented and beautiful and strong. She's been through so much, Dad. And I fucked it up."

"Then fix it."

"How?"

"If you love her," he says softly, "you'll figure it out."

I hear a noise below me. It's the service door. My heart stops as Bree appears from under the terrace. Oh my god. Has she been here the whole fucking time?

My heart leaps into my throat as she walks toward the beach. She's alone. A moonlit silhouette.

"I have to go," I say.

"Where are you going?"

"I really love her, and I think I just figured it out."

I hang up and turn around. And screech to a halt. The guys are all lined up at the windows and in the open doorway, watching me like I'm an exhibit at the zoo. I'd be embarrassed if I weren't suddenly frantic.

"Where's the dog?" I yell.

Grady lets out a nervous laugh for the whole group. "Dude, we know you and your girlfriend broke up, but dogs are illegal and shit."

I flip him off and march forward. A first-year pushes through the clog of bodies, Matilda outstretched in his hands. "Here."

I take the wiggling dog in my arms and whip back around.

"Where the hell are you going?" Grady yells for the second time tonight.

I ignore him and jog down the tiered steps. Bree has disappeared from my view, but I know where she's going.

I reach the sand and set down the dog. "Go get me that bra."

Matilda takes off and I follow, running as fast as I can in the heavy sand.

My phone dings with a text, and I stumble, falling to a knee. I pull the phone from my pocket. It's Dad again. *Aces pick is next. Answer the phone.*

I stand and keep running to the top of the dune.

Bree turns around. She looks at Matilda, confusion coloring her expression. She drops to her knees and picks up the dog and hugs it to her chest.

Then she sees me.

Stands.

Freezes.

I force my feet to move. The phone rings again.

I ignore it.

"What are you doing here?" Bree whispers when I reach her.

I can barely answer. Her eyes are puffy and red, and my stomach turns inside out, because I'm the cause. I want to haul her to me and kiss her until she has no more doubts about how I feel. Now and always.

My phone rings. I hold her gaze while I lift the screen for her to read it.

"Who is it?" I ask.

Her eyes get wide and round as she looks back up at me. "It says Las Vegas."

I shove the phone in my pocket.

"Jax, are you crazy? You have to answer that."

"No, I don't."

Her head starts to shake. "Jax, no. This is the first round! What are you doing?"

What am I doing?

I'm breaking the fucking rules.

I'm risking everything.

Because when she locks those watery brown eyes with mine, I know it's going to be worth it.

Bree always is.

32

BREE

MY HEART IS GOING to explode. Matilda wiggles against me and tries to lick my chin, and only then do I realize it's wet. Wet with tears I didn't even know are running down my face.

I've missed him so much. I'm shredded inside, broken. I came out here to get some air because I knew the draft had started, and I couldn't stand not being with him.

But here he is.

Ignoring the phone.

Staring at me like the sun rises and sets in me alone.

"Jax," I whisper, because his name is the only word I can get past the emotion in my throat.

He closes the distance between us and takes Matilda from my arms. He sets her down and, miraculously, she lays down at my feet. Like this was her plan all along.

Jax cups my face in his hands. "The first night we came here, I knew nothing about you. I thought I did. I knew you were the most beautiful girl I'd ever seen. I knew I'd never felt about anyone the way I felt when I looked at you. And not because I felt sorry for you or because I'm a therapy dog who wants to shove my face in your armpit."

I blink. "What?"

He shakes his head. "It doesn't matter. The point is, I didn't really know you, and I screwed it all up, and I let you get away."

His phone dings with a voicemail alert.

"Jax, stop. You have to check that."

He ignores me. "And here we are. Two years later, and I'm still screwing it up. But it's worse, because I really know you now. Not just beautiful Bree who dances on the beach. Not just stubborn Bree who sleeps in a closet. I know the real you. The good and the bad. And I don't care who is on that phone. I don't care what they have to offer me."

I suck in a shaky breath. What is he doing? What is he saying?

The callused pads of his thumbs caress my cheekbones. "I was terrified of who I was without baseball, but what scares me more than anything is who I am without you. I can survive without the game. I can't survive without you."

I circle his wrists with my fingers. I have so much I need to say, but his phone rings again.

He ignores it.

"Jax, answer it."

He tugs me closer. "I should have held you last night when you tried to push me away. I should have told you I'm in this with you for the long haul."

I start to shake everywhere.

"Bree, I want to play Major League baseball."

"Then answer the phone!" I sob.

"But I don't want it without you. There is no path that my life takes that is complete if you're not on it with me."

My chest bursts. "I'm so sorry, Jax. I was scared. I don't know how to do this. I don't know how to trust people. I don't how to swing at curve balls."

He laughs. "What?"

I shake my head. "It doesn't matter. There is no path that my life takes that I don't want for you—want you to be..." I stop and groan. "Whatever you just said. Ditto."

He laughs and presses his forehead to mine. "No matter who is calling me, no matter where I go, I'm with you. And no matter where you end up with the Beckinsale thing, I'm with you. We will make it work."

I nod. Overcome. Tears drip from my chin. He slides his hands around my head and weaves his fingers into my hair. I've never seen him like this before. Complete. Peaceful.

"When was the last time someone told you that you're the most important thing in the world to them?" he whispers.

"Never," I whisper.

"That ends today."

Then he kisses me. He devours me. Savors me. I cling to him. Tears from both our eyes dampen our cheeks, drip down our faces. He wraps me in his arms.

His phone rings again.

He pulls back, and my heart swells at the look in his eyes, and I know.

This is how it starts for us.

A sandy beach. A moonlit lake. A ten-pound ball of white fluff and sass at our feet.

And a ringing phone.

"I love you, Bree McTavish. *Forever*."

I choke on a sob and a laugh. "I love you, Jax Tanner. Forever. Now will you please answer that?"

EPILOGUE

THREE MONTHS LATER

"YOU KNOW, at some point, you will have to actually open your eyes when he plays."

I keep my hands over my face. "I can't, Lexi. What if he strikes out because of me?"

It wasn't supposed to happen this fast. He was supposed to play in the minors for at least a year. That's what he told me. What everyone told me. Even a first-round draft pick with a two million dollar signing bonus has to play in the minors for a while, but the Aces called him up to fill in for a player on the disabled list. It might just be for one game against the Detroit Tigers, but it could be longer.

I barely had time to get an absence cleared by my instructors in Nashville—I chose that because it was closest to the Memphis team he was assigned to—before jumping on a plane to get here in time.

Now I'm sitting in the family section of Comerica Park with his parents and Lexi, and I'm wearing an Aces jersey with his name on the back. And I'm too scared to watch.

I feel a hand pat my knee. "It will get easier," his mom says.

His family is so warm and lovely, and I knew the minute I met them why Jax is the way he is. They're a whole family of golden retrievers who met me with tails wagging.

"What's happening?" I ask.

"Open your eyes and see for yourself," Lexi says.

I pull one hand away. Then the other.

"You're still closing your eyes," Lexi says.

I crack open one eye. Jax stands a foot away from the plate, rolling the bat in his gloved hands. His Aces uniform hugs every inch of him, and I feel faint. I love him so much. How can he be so calm? So confident?

Jax takes his stance at the plate.

The ball leaves the pitcher's hands.

I open my other eye as Jax swings.

And sends the curve ball flying over the wall.

ABOUT LYSSA KAY ADAMS

Lyssa Kay Adams is a Rita-nominated romance writer and diehard Detroit Tigers fan who will occasionally cheer for the Red Sox because her husband is from Boston. Her debut novel, *Seventh Inning Heat*, was released in March 2016 and is the first in a series about a fictional baseball team, The Vegas Aces. Her novella, *Wild in Rio*, was nominated for a prestigious Rita Award--the highest distinction in romance fiction--by Romance Writers of America. She lives in Michigan with her husband, daughter, and a pesky, ten-pound ball of white fluff who may or may not be the inspiration for Matilda in *The Prospect*.

THANKS FOR READING!

I love connecting with my readers! Connect with me on Face-book and Twitter. Or sign up here to be among the first to hear about my new releases, contests, and the antics of my very own pesky white ball of fluff.

Want to read more? Check out LyssaKayAdams.com for information on my other books!

Made in the USA
Las Vegas, NV
19 March 2021

19831172R00104